Magic Hooves

and

Ghostly Clues

MIMI SINGER

Advanced Scientific Communications

Contents

Chapter 1

I bang on the letterbox with my fist to dislodge any tarantulas that might have made their home in it before I open its flap at the back. Luckily, no rent-free wildlife squatters attack my fingers. The promised envelope with the keys is meant to tell me more about my new home away from home.

There is a ring with two keys on it; a large iron key for the front door and a new modern back door key.

Printed on 'Green Bowlder Equine Hospital' letterhead, complete with the green logo of two horse heads, is a note to me.

"Dear Miss Clay,
Welcome to Green Bowlder Vet Hospital!
As discussed by phone, this house is provided
for your use for the next three months.
You are required to be on-site a couple of times
each week be on-site during the night from
6:00 pm to 7:00 am to render assistance to any

client who needs the hospital between those hours.

As agreed, you have the use of the stable with its yard, and a small paddock for one horse only. We will not provide food for that horse.

We provide a parking spot for your car in the hospital carpark.

You can reach the hospital either via the driveway and the main gate (by car) or on foot via the brick path that leads directly to the building from the back door of your house.

I expect to see you tomorrow morning at 8:00 am.

Leonard Scott. Principal Veterinarian.

"George, this sounds so formal," I say, slightly nervous, to my black and tan Kelpie on the passenger seat.

The driveway to the 'house' is dimpled by prize-winning potholes that make the horse trailer hitch behind my SUV clunk, and my horse inside scrambles.

"Oh, my, George. I think Leonard has grossly exaggerated. This house is about the smallest house I've ever seen. It can barely be called a cottage. But it looks so cute; I love it anyway! I think we will be happy here."

The old weatherboard cottage with its rusty tin roof is well past its prime but not quite ready to be pulled down.

Once painted in a cheery yellow, its color now reminds me of calf diarrhea or baby poo.

The front porch beams and the window frames are painted dark green, reminiscent of ancient country train stations. Flecks of drifted grass seeds embedded in spiderwebs have gathered in the paint cracks for months, or maybe years.

It looks tired, but not haunted by ghosts or bats.

Driving closer and taking in the general feel of the place, a welcoming committee of one blocks my way. A calico cat sits right in the middle of the drive, where it splits around the round garden bed in front of the cottage. There is no way I can pass without first acknowledging the cat that stops me from taking over 'her property'.

The silence, as I stop the SUV and step out, feels overwhelming after the six-hour drive.

"Stay, George."

"Hello, cat!" I stoop to the tricolor cat, which sits there like an Egyptian statue, staring at me with orange eyes. Any cat lover would adore a cat with eyes like that.

The feline goddess does not make any move to accept my greetings. I stretch my hand toward her left cheek to offer respectful friendliness, but she is having none of it. Her brows show doubt, and her whiskers move forward to measure my hands for a potential toothy reprimand.

I pull my hand back, but she still doesn't move.

"What is this, 'Cat with the orange eyes and royal bearing'? Are you the gatekeeper of this ancient palace?"

The cat looks at me with ageless wisdom in her golden eyes, stands up, yawns, and, after a leisurely stretch, turns toward the cottage. Her measured steps around the garden bed island are unhurried and calm. She keeps her tail low behind her, not high like a flagpole. She's not inviting me to become her friend.

Arriving on the porch before me, she plants herself on the doormat outside the front door.

The big old key fits, and the door opens without creaking.

"Ouff!" I say to the cat. "This air smells old."

The front door leads directly into a small living room with a tiny cast-iron fireplace. The window to the driveway allows the dust to dance in the horizontal rays of the late afternoon sun.

On the right, a door leads to what I think is the master bedroom. A queen-sized bed with a modern green bed cover looks inviting. I'm surprised at how comfortable it feels once I sit on it. The sash window looks out to the driveway, its curtains thin and almost see-through.

This is a new bed bought for the intern to help her feel comfortable. *Thank you, Leonard, I appreciate it.*

The cat wanders toward a door at the back of the living room. I open it to a short, dark corridor that leads to the back door. To the right, a door leads into a tiny second bedroom.

She waits for me to open the kitchen door to the left. The bathroom, a recent addition to the cottage, is on the right, next to the back door.

"Ha, you're hungry?"

The cat ignores me as I open the new fridge, relieved that there is no decaying meat or moldy bread that needs to be disposed of to make room for my food.

The wooden cupboards along the kitchen wall open and shut with a time-worn clunk. A huge wooden dining table dominates the kitchen. Any city restaurant would pay top dollar for the authentic wear and tear. The oven is old, but I avoid cooking as much as I can, so I am not fussed about its age.

"This table is fantastic," I say to the cat. "Who are we going to invite for dinner here, hmm? In this deserted place, that's not likely to happen."

Still, she says nothing.

I open the back door, Leonard's letter in hand, to walk along the brick path toward the hospital building. It winds through a completely overgrown garden to a small gate in a tall Lillypilly hedge.

At least I know where to go in the morning.

"Let's put Princess to bed before it gets dark," I say to the cat who has followed me.

The stable, a small weatherboard shed without windows, also ancient-yellow, with an overhanging roof, allows space for one horse. The tack room brings tears to my eyes. The old, faint smell of horses reminds me of Pony Club and the romance of ponies and girls brushing and doting on them. A tie-up rail opposite a gate next to the tack room leads into a yard behind the stable.

"This will do nicely," I mumble into the fading afternoon light.

Princess unloads from the float and follows me into the stall as if she already knows the place. The water trough in the yard is full of clean water. I flake off a couple of hay biscuits from the hay bale on the bed of my SUV and drop them in her yard.

"Good night, Princess. See you in the morning." I gently stroke her gray flea-bitten white coat and the half-moon-shaped scar on her forehead.

Princess nickers softly as I leave to unload my own belongings into the cottage.

George jumps out of the car, pushing past the cat and giving me 'The Look'. How could I forget him in the car? He scampers around her, sniffing out our new home, both inside and outside.

"It's ok, George. Dinner will be ready in a minute."

The bag of dog food and the freezer box goes in the kitchen and now there are just four more cardboard boxes that hold pantry items and my veterinary textbooks. I pile my favorite family and horse photos on the dresser in my bedroom. There will be time tomorrow to hang them up properly.

Mum has thrown a pile of winter coats and hanging bags with my long dresses on the back seat. Fat chance I will wear them here, but the puffer jacket will come in handy, considering the miniature fireplace in the cottage. I may need to wear it to bed at night.

Under the pile of garments sits a green metal trunk, strapped in by the seatbelt. I can't remember packing it, but I put it with the other boxes on the big dining table.

"Come on inside!" I hold the cottage door open for the cat and George.

The cat ignores me and stays on the doormat, staring into the darkness across the garden bed; I wonder what she sees.

George doesn't wait for a second invitation and darts into the kitchen, waiting for his bowl of kibble.

Time to call Mum.

Chapter 2

To my surprise, there is good reception here.

"Have you unpacked yet?" says Mum as if unpacking was the most important thing to do.

"Not yet. I just took all the boxes inside. The place is a little spooky but also very cute. I am too tired now and just want to relax. I'm a little anxious about tomorrow. I feel so not ready, Mum."

"Don't they let you have a day to settle in before you start work?"

"No, I start straightaway. There is a letter here with details."

"Did you find Nan's box? The green metal box with the lock. I put the key on your car key bunch."

"That box! I wondered what it was."

"Go through it tonight. There may be some useful tools for you that Nan used when she treated horses."

"She was a great horse whisperer, and I loved her very much. But today, we use drugs that are so much more powerful than those of Nan's time."

"But she also has notebooks that might be useful; just have a look. At least it will remind you of Nan and her interest in horse medicine. And it's something that will connect you to home. Promise?"

"Promise," I say as I stare at the old, scratched box with its ancient shipping labels plastered all over. Nan must have traveled a lot when she was younger. Why didn't she ever tell me anything about where she had been?

"I am so looking forward to starting. In the advertisement, it mentioned that I would be one of six 'enthusiastic vets in a bustling work environment'. I'll call you tomorrow after work, Mum." I say and click off.

Let's make some tea first.

The water pipes stutter and sputter, as expected, so I let the rusty water run out into the sink until it is clear. Tank water and rusty pipes. Great.

While I wait for the kettle to boil, I carry Nan's green metal trunk to the living room. It's heavy and probably full of antique books that should be in a museum. I might put them on the bookshelves in the living room that already house a small collection of old books.

The key on my car ring opens the trunk. There are, in fact, books in it and a folder with documents. On top of it all sits a twitch.

"A twitch! Everyone who owns a horse knows how to use one to keep an uncooperative horse calm." I imagine placing the rope loop over Princess' soft upper lip, then twisting the stick to compress her lip. The squeezing signals the horse's brain to release calming endorphins.

It seems to be the only 'gadget' in the box. "I suppose I can always use a twitch," I mutter.

It has a dark brown wooden handle with intricate carving from the rope loop to its other end. The carved handle is shiny from Nan's hands and maybe some other hands before her time. The carved lines and contours of the number 1870 have faded from age and use, but they remain readable, and the rope is still sturdy and sleek.

This must be ancient. I'll clip it on my belt in the morning to keep it handy.

Right under the twitch, I find a letter addressed to me, not one of those antiquated letters sealed with wax, but a plain letter in an ordinary white envelope.

> *"Dear Riona,*
> *You found this letter, so you must have opened the green trunk.*
> *There is no need to examine everything all at once. Take your time. You might find the notebooks useful if you have an open mind, especially my notes and books on plants and how to make potions and lotions.*
> *Take care of the jewelry pieces. They will give*

you a unique energy when you wear them.
The crystals will help you once you learn how
and when to use them. Be careful and use the
book of spells wisely! Accept and appreciate
your powers.
I pass my twitch on to you. It was very dear to
me and has helped me deal with many difficult
horses.
You will discover its special powers, and in
time, it will become your magic wand.
Stay safe and open your mind to the spirit
guides of the universe who will help and sup-
port you.
Your adoring grandmother,
Anastasia."

That's typical Grandma, always bringing the universe into the discussion.

With less curiosity than Nan would have expected, I briefly rummage through the box. There is an old newspaper, its few frayed pages apparently read many times.

"The Paranormal Monthly."

Far out! Did Nan read paranormal stuff? I'm astonished, but she mentioned the universe and spirit guides in her letter. It's odd that I didn't know she believed so much in the paranormal.

I take note of a stack of letters held together by a faded, once-red ribbon, notebooks labeled according to years, a book on spells and plants, and a few photos in picture frames.

A delicate silver jewelry case holds colorful crystals, gemstones - which are probably fake - a necklace, and brooches.

I stack everything back into the trunk except the twitch. I will read the letters one day, once I have settled in here, I promise myself.

"Another cup of tea, George?"

When I return to the living room, the tricolor cat is washing her face on the coffee table.

Spirit guides. If the universe and the spirit guides had done their job, I wouldn't have ended up in a ditch under my horse and in a coma for a month. Rehab for a year wasn't a picnic either, so much for the help of spirit guides.

"Rrrreow, Reooow!"

The cat stares at my face, eyes black and round as if ready to attack.

"How did you get in? And what got into you? Are you supposed to be one of those spirit guides?"

She wearily blinks at me once and then turns away to carefully groom her ears.

"I see. You can communicate with me. Any comment? How do you think I am supposed to understand what you are telling me, cat? In case you are a spirit guide."

The cat ignores me. Was my question stupid?

After storing all the food that Mum had packed into the freezer and the pantry, I collapse in my bed, painfully aware of the metal screws and plates holding my body together. The covers are soft and warm, and the number of pillows is just right for me. George doesn't wait for an invitation to hop on the bed and curls up at my feet.

Before I switch off the reading lamp on my bedside table, I glance at the large oil painting on the wall to my right. An old woman sitting on a green upholstered chair like those in the living room beside the fireplace. Her eyes look older than old, wise but resigned to the sadness of a difficult life.

I wonder who she is. Maybe she owned the cottage once.

Tomorrow, I'll move her picture into the second bedroom. Now, I can only hope my body recovers enough from the drive to function for my first day at work.

Chapter 3

The loud warble of magpies in the gum trees around the cottage penetrates my dream of Nan telling me to wake up. It's six o'clock, far too early to be awake. My body hurts and feels way past its use-by date. I gingerly stretch and bend my joints before planting my feet on the creaking pine floorboards.

"Oh, my! How am I going to survive a whole day of work? I feel so broken." George doesn't care; he simply wants to be let out.

I shuffle to the kitchen to put the kettle on and grind enough coffee for two cups. The cat is nowhere to be seen. I wonder what her name is. They'll tell me at the clinic, I guess.

After feeding Princess her breakfast, a small cup full of pellets, and two some hay, I take a shower and slip into my work gear, blue jeans, a blue polo shirt, and my brown Blundstone boots.

"You've got to stay here, George. It's my first day. I'll have to find out if you can come to the clinic or on outside calls before I take you with me."

I lock him up in the oversized kennel outside the backdoor. A water bowl and his breakfast should keep him happy until I come home from work.

"Stay safe, Princess. I'll be back soon," I yell at the horse, and she answers back with a trumpeting neigh as I turn toward the path from the backdoor to the clinic.

"What about the twitch? You promised!" I hear Grandma's voice in my mind.

"I can't remember promising anything, Nan," I mumble, as if she were real, but rush back inside to clip the twitch on my belt by its rope loop. It feels a little uncomfortable, swinging next to my left thigh as I walk. Never mind, I will either get used to it, or I'll leave it at home in future.

The weather couldn't be any better for my first day at work, a mid-autumn day, blue sky, and crisp morning air before a warm midday and afternoon.

I am awed by the enormous clinic building, with its sandstone walls and galvanized iron roof. A row of gigantic water tanks is lined up near a seemingly never-ending hedge of cypress trees. They'll have enough water for years of firefighting, on top of what they need to run the hospital.

A row of parked SUVs shows me there are other human beings here. Let the bustling begin!

With a resolute flair, I open the reception door and offer a friendly greeting.

Behind the counter, a head with dark, sleek, tied-back hair and black-framed glasses pops up.

She could be a carbon copy of Ruth Bader Ginsburg, I think. But then, this person likely doesn't even know who RBG is.

"I'm Riona. Today is my first day here."

"Hi Riona, I'm Amy. I'll call Leonard, he'll introduce you to the others. He'll have the contract for you to sign, too," she says.

On the dot of 8 o'clock, Leonard appears, a middle-aged, sour-faced man, maybe in his late fifties.

He stretches his hand out to me.

"You're Riona, the new intern? Glad you found the place. Is the cottage satisfactory? My wife prepared everything for you."

"It wasn't hard to find," I reply, shaking his hand. He reminds me of an overfed Hereford bull with his chunky torso and arms as thick as my thighs. His short-sleeved shirt bulges over his muscles and especially his round belly, showing black hair through the gaps between the buttons. A black leather belt under said round belly holds up his mid-thigh long shorts.

I try not to focus on the bald spot on the top of his head. I am about two or three hands taller than he is and half his width.

Not my type of male. My mind is putting him into the category of 'Ugly and not to be trifled with'.

"I'm Leonard Scott. I own the hospital with my wife. We built it up from scratch some fifteen years ago. But before I give you a guided tour, I have a question for you."

"Yes?"

"Do you think you will be up to it? I mean, going into full-time vet practice after your accident? It will be full-on. If not here at the hospital, then outside with clients. Do you still have to do rehab?"

I generally avoid talking about the accident because it was my fault that it happened. Remembering that I had inspected this Trakehner jump the day before and thought it might frighten the horse, I hesitated during the last few strides toward it, thinking of what could go wrong instead of taking it on the way I should have. After that it was lights out for me for a month.

How we ended up upside down was captured on enough mobile phones and so widely distributed on YouTube that it allowed me to analyze it once I'd come out of the induced coma. Now, I have enough metal screws and plates in my spine, and other places, to set off any airport scanner.

Unfortunately, the horse had to be put down because of her injuries, but everybody kept that a secret until I was in rehab. They also kept from me that my favorite grandmother, Mum's mother, had died from a heart attack the same day I had the accident.

In hindsight, I was glad I hadn't known that until later because I would have wanted to die too, instead of fighting for life; I loved her so much. People called her a horse whisperer and a horse witch because she could fix horse behaviors and explain to the owners why they had developed.

So here I am, supposedly free of all worries, hoping for a new beginning after recovering from my accident and mastering all the required rehab steps. How can I convince this man that he doesn't need to worry about my capabilities?

"No, I don't need to do rehab anymore, and, of course, I'm up to it. I wouldn't have applied for the internship if I had any doubts."

He scans my body from top to toe for potential shortcomings, and I feel the blood rush to my face.

I wonder if he knows I've applied dozens of times for internships but was knocked back every time.

"Well, it's for three months, for now. We'll see how you go and then we can make up our minds if we continue your internship.

Chapter 4

I've never lacked confidence. Dad always encouraged me to be bold and have a go, especially when I had doubts. In his eyes, I am his gorgeous girl and can do anything I face.

When I was younger, people said I would grow into my arms and legs, though they're still too long for regular pants and long-sleeved tops. What annoyed me more were comments about how I would grow into my teeth. My upper "fangs" were said to be oversized and took a long time to grow down. After a torturous few years fitted with hardware in my mouth, I now have 'regular' teeth.

Even though I'm twenty-four years old, I haven't grown the correct number of curves in the right places to be 'pleasing to the eye'. People who wish me ill say I look scrawny, too tall, and have an unflattering long blond ponytail, more suited to the backend of a Clydesdale.

Facing my new boss, I wish I had more confidence in myself and my knowledge. I feel like a fake in Blund-stones.

Leonard's scan of my body ends with a resigned sigh.

"Now, follow me, and you can introduce yourself to the others."

Leonard shows me the facilities, the envy of any university veterinary hospital, with the profession's newest and most expensive tools. The laboratory is equipped with microscopes and blood analysis machines, tanks with frozen horse semen, and, of course, an impressive operating theatre.

He shows me the stable block with a central breezeway and horse crushes, and I am duly impressed with those, too, even though the stables are empty. He leads me outside to a round yard next to the Cypress hedge.

"This is a beautiful horse," I say about the black thoroughbred stallion in the yard.

"Yes, he is beautiful. That is Black Lightning, better known as Barracuda, for obvious reasons. He is our breeding stallion for thoroughbred racehorses. He will be busy in the breeding season, but now is his time off."

"Impressive!" The stallion stares at us both but does not move a muscle to come close for a pat. Barracuda. I understand.

"Now, I'll let Amy do the introductions to our staff; I need to attend to other business. Congratulations, and welcome to our team."

Amy is in no hurry to lead me to the staff room. I'm bothered by the noise of her heels dragging on the polished concrete, but her tight jeans are hindering her ability to walk with enthusiasm. On the way up the stairs to the staff room, I stumble but catch myself on the handrail.

Five young women and an Asian man get up from their comfortable chairs to greet me. They all wear jeans and dark blue T-shirts with the hospital logo on their chest and back.

"Hi, nice to meet you; I'm Riona," I say as their eyes assess my fitness as a horse vet intern.

After a brief shake of hands, I find out that they are a vet nurse and four of the five vets who work here.

The nurse, Lorna, is short but looks strong and almost bursting out of her dark blue overalls. She leaves for the stable, and I acquaint myself with the vets.

Nerida, Janice, and Molly are all in their thirties. They've been working at the hospital for over three years and say they enjoy life in the country. They live nearby and promise to visit me at the cottage soon to help me feel part of the family.

Nerida, the tallest of the three women, is not quite as tall as I am but at least thirty kilos heavier and well-muscled. She has the annoying habit of laughing at the end of every sentence that leaves her mouth. Irritating. She looks at me suspiciously, as if I'm not strong enough for a job as a horse vet. Unlike her gym-trained body, mine is somewhat thin. The term scrawny crosses my mind again, but I dismiss it immediately.

Get over your lack of confidence!

Molly gushes about the wonderful facilities and the great support she got when she started, like me, as an intern. Janice is shorter than Molly and seems genuinely friendly. She is responsible for any small animals that come into the clinic and has her own consult room and operating theater. But she has no patients yet today.

Lei is a vet from Hong Kong, an intern on invitation for a few months. He is quite formal in his language and demeanor. I find him hard to read as he doesn't visibly convey any emotions.

"What's your accent?" asks Molly. "Are you Dutch?"

"No, I'm Australian, but I spent a year in Germany. So it must have rubbed off on me."

"So, we have two with accents. We're almost outnumbered," she laughs.

Nerida picks up her car keys from the staff room table and turns toward the door.

"Why don't you come with me this morning for outside calls? That will give you the lay of the land, and you'll meet some of our wonderful clients, hehehe."

"Sure," I say.

Nerida grabs a few supplies from the pharmacy cupboards to stock the trays of her white SUV.

"Let's go," she says, her excitement slightly over the top, and laughs as if the most sensational cases in veterinary practice were awaiting us. The laugh annoys me. What's so funny about 'let's go'?

It is true, though; I do learn the lay of the land. Straight roads, crossed by other straight roads, crisscrossing the undulating basalt landscape. Fortunately, the GPS is working, and all the crossroads have signs.

"There are no horse patients here at the hospital. I thought it would be busier." Maybe I can clear up the mystery of the non-bustling horse hospital.

"Yeah, that sometimes happens. It's not exactly peak season for horses now. They enjoy the late summer before the wet autumn weather sets in. The breeding season won't start for a while. So, enjoy the easy life for a bit." She laughs again.

I nod. Maybe she's right. If I go on some calls, I'll learn more without being left to my own devices. Speaking of devices, none of the vets made a comment about my twitch, which is still clipped to my belt.

Chapter 5

Wt arrive at a dilapidated farm to see a lame horse. The old farmer is obviously lame, too, as he leads us slowly to a small yard next to a shed where an old horse stands in his dark shelter. Head droopy, it looks even older than its owner. Both seem a little neglected, one with holes in his boots, the other with dreadlocks in his mane.

After Nerida introduces me as the new addition to the vet team, he leads the horse out into the farmyard so we can assess its lameness. The horse limps on three legs.

"Oh-oh," says Nerida. "You are very sore." She tries to touch the horse's lame left front foot while the farmer holds the horse by its halter. But the horse is not cooperative. It spins around its owner on three feet, nimbler than the old man.

"Would you mind, Riona, twitching the horse as you have your twitch handy, hehehehe?"

I approach the horse with my twitch, pat his neck, and speak to him in a soothing voice.

"Good boy, you are in so much pain. Let me slip this over your lip, and you will not feel a thing, I promise." I slip the rope loop over his upper lip.

The carved wooden handle lies snugly in my left hand as I twist it, and the old horse stops huffing. He calms to a standstill as the warmth of my hands spreads around his body.

"Good boy," I say. "You see, this works, and you will be fine after Nerida checks your foot. It might just be a foot abscess."

The wooden handle of the twitch hums in my hand, and the horse relaxes.

Nerida gets busy and checks out the horse's foot.

"Yes, it's quite hot. Let me clean out the hoof first and see whether it really is a foot abscess."

She scrapes away the dirt and then cuts away the overgrown hoof.

"Yes, it is a foot abscess, but it's close to bursting. I'll open it to let it drain."

She keeps chiseling away at the horse's sole until it suddenly flinches when she reaches the abscess.

"There we go. There is a lot of pus. We'll bandage it for a few days to keep the dirt out. Riona, you can let the twitch go. He'll tolerate the bandaging without it."

I loosen the twitch, and the horse licks his lip, grimacing to test whether it still works. He then rubs his face on my shoulder.

"You're welcome, boy."

I return the lead rope to the owner and help Nerida bandage the foot.

After confirming that the clinic has the client's payment details, there is a quick goodbye, and we're off again.

Hooray, I think. This marks my first case as a horse vet intern, even though I was merely employing the twitch to pacify a horse. It's not impressive, but it's at least a beginning.

Nerida floors the gas pedal and roars out of the yard, almost taking the gate post with us. What is wrong with her?

"You could have at least waited with your diagnosis until I had investigated the foot. Next time, be a bit more considerate of my professional feelings. I am competent and don't need to be upstaged by a complete newbie." This time, she leaves out her irritating laugh at the end of her statement.

I stay silent, but in my mind, I note the signs of jealousy. On the next call, Nerida orders me to twitch a yearling with a cut above his knee while she stitches the wound. At the third call, she asks me to fetch a tub of medication out of the car's medicine drawer for a calf with diarrhea. The irritating laugh after each order sounds insane and out of place to me.

We're out of each appointment in minimum time. Nerida makes a detour to a racehorse stud and training stable, where she unloads twelve white tubs with blue lids into a giant letterbox. I dare not ask what they contain. She must know this road well because she navigates the potholes silently and at a speed I don't feel comfortable with. My dislike of her increases with each bump in the road.

I'm sure I've made an enemy for life. But I'll actually only be here for three months. After that, we won't need to put up with each other anymore.

In the clinic car park, she slams the driver's door and disappears toward the staff room.

Shaking my body into a workable configuration, I leave the car and relax my mind. I must say I love this twitch. It's the first and only one that hums in my hand when it's connected with a horse's body. Maybe it is a magic twitch, after all.

The only addition to the row of parked vehicles is a shiny Ford Ranger Raptor, midnight blue with black trim. The enormous bull bar at the front, searchlights, and an oversized antenna on the roof ooze excessive levels of testosterone. The side doors of the custom-fitted hold-all in the bed are lifted, ready for restocking its shelves. The enormous tires are made for off-roading, but not a speck of dust or grime ruins this manifestation of masculinity. It probably has never seen a bush track.

This must belong to the fifth vet. It can only be a man who drives such a massive macho SUV.

I stride through the stable block's breezeway, checking to see if any new patients have moved in while we were out, but there are none.

Opening the reception door, I see him. The fifth vet, leaning over the counter toward Amy, his curly blond hair almost touching her face. I can only see him from behind: booted ankles crossed, a sturdy, expensive leather belt holding up deliberately tight denim shorts. His musclebound back and shoulders in the clinic tee look gym-enhanced. Impressive! Leonard must like over-exercised people like Nerida and this super-male. It figures someone like that drives the Ranger Raptor outside.

He hears the reception door clang shut and turns.

"Riona!"

My heart drops to the bottom of my stomach. Blood rushes to my head. I can't believe it. Michael, my nemesis from my first year of vet school in Sydney. I am speechless.

"What are you doing here?" he says, all smiles. "I thought you were dead. Glad you're not." The familiar cheek and chin dimples have deepened and may even have been enhanced by a plastic surgeon.

His eyes wander over every part of my body, lingering on my chest. He hasn't changed a bit, the lecher.

"I'm the new intern, and I'll be working here for the next three months." I leave it at that.

Amy looks at me with pitying eyes.

"Has Leonard signed my contract yet?" I ask, striving to keep it neutral.

"You'll be lucky if you get it in the next month. Olga is doing all the paperwork." laughs Michael.

"Who's Olga?"

"Leonard's wife. Make sure you don't cross her because she'll make your life a misery. So, if you are the new intern, you live in the cottage?"

Even though it sounds like a question, I can see the little wheels in his brain work, concluding that I am only a few minutes away from his grasp.

"Yes, I do live there—with my dog and my horse."

"And the vicious cat. She'll be your best protector out there." He laughs, giving me another once-over with his eyes, stopping at my chest again with a disappointed sigh.

"You haven't changed a bit. I'll come over in the next few days to explain how we work here."

He disappears into the staffroom, his booming laugh and the obliging chiming in of the females sounding dismissive behind the thin walls that hold no secrets.

Amy gives me another pitiful look.

"You two know each other?"

"Yes," I say, leaving out the word 'unfortunately'. "We started in the same year in Sydney. He was the biggest womanizer I have ever met. Saying no in college was like an aphrodisiac to him, but he didn't get me. I was one of the few who stood up to him, but it was hard. I hope he's changed."

Amy rolls her eyes and snorts through her throat. Her silence speaks volumes.

"You can have lunch at your cottage until three o'clock when there's an outside call. But maybe Michael or Molly will take it."

I dash out, my legs still shaking, along the windy brick path to the cottage.

Chapter 6

The cat sits next to the dog kennel at the backdoor, waiting for me to let George out. Her golden eyes gleam like Baltic amber in the sunlight.

"Hi, vicious cat."

She stands up and lifts her tail like a flagpole.

"Mrrrr," she says.

"You like being called 'Vicious'?"

She trots through the back door into the kitchen, followed by George. Princess neighs at me from her yard.

"Yes, yes, let me make a sandwich, and I'll come over for lunch."

Vicious has parked herself on the kitchen table and looks like a loaf of bread, her front paws tucked under her body.

"Do you want something? I don't have any cat food, but I can give you some cheese. Maybe this afternoon, I'll buy some food for you if we drive past the town."

She pretends not to hear me. After all, she cared for herself before I arrived here.

Grabbing my cup of tea and sandwich, I wander to Princess' stable, where I sit down on the chair that has probably been there forever. The sun is bearable and the flies less so, but I need the company of Princess. George is out and about sniffing the surroundings, happy in his own world.

I ponder how to deal with Michael turning up in my life again—unwanted as ever. The one-year battle to keep him at bay at college took its toll on me. The derogatory remarks and putdowns were relentless. He and his friends enjoyed calling me names.

Taking a gap year, traveling to horse studs throughout Europe, gave me enough confidence to go back to University. After graduation came the accident, and it was like lights out for a whole year. Michael had been obliterated from my memory, until now.

I feel the cat brush against my leg.

"Hi, Vicious," I say, stroking her back, which ripples under my hand. She turns for another pat, and I feel the purr rumbling in her throat, a deep purr for such a small cat.

Life feels good suddenly. I know I'll cope for the next three months.

After a while, I get up with a bit of stiffness that reminds me too much of all the hardware in my body and the bumpy road with Nerida.

After rinsing my cup and plate, I place them into the dish rack. There is still time to put away some of my belongings and connect my laptop to the internet. But where is the modem?

Opening cupboard after cupboard, I finally find it behind a concealed door in the wood paneling of the living room. Vicious pointed at the hidden button for opening it with her eyes. She must like hiding places.

There are a few mostly empty shelves in this compartment, and the inside of the door is covered by an old map from 1920. It appears to be a map of the property with its boundaries marked. I can see that there is a mansion somewhere, a Green Bowlder Lane that leads to a B W Cottage, and lines marking other landscape features. The cottage is a tiny speck on a property that covers a vast area. I must compare it to Google Earth. I find the login details on the modem and switch it on. Bingo! I am live and can talk to anyone on the planet.

It is almost three o'clock, so I rush to shut the cupboard. The cat sits in the doorway of the little room, staring at a painting on the floor that is leaning against its back wall.

"What is it, Vicious, or should I call you Precious?"

I pull the painting out and blow the dust off its gold-gilded wooden frame. Old and a little faded, it's otherwise in good condition.

"That should go over the fireplace, Precious."

It's not too heavy, and with a bit of fiddling of the wire at its back, the painting finally hangs above the fireplace.

I step back and look at the face of a young woman in a three-quarter-length art nouveau-style dress. Her blond hair is cropped into a wavy bob and covered by a tight cap. She looks at me as if asking questions or inviting me to a conversation.

"I wonder who that is, Precious, but there's no time to find out now. I need to get back to work."

After putting the reluctant George back in the dog run, I rush back to the clinic.

Only a small Kia, I assume Amy's, and the muscle car are in the car park. Everyone else is out. Michael leans on the driver's door like an advertisement for Ford Raptors.

"Does it always take you so long to put your face on? I was just about to pick you up for our tete-a-tete this afternoon. Get in. No time to lose."

"There is no tete-a-tete," I say. "What case are we going to?"

"Our most important racehorse clients. We need to do some blood work for them before the races this week-end and tell them how to adjust their treatments."

The Raptor is more comfortable than I thought. Michael fills me in on the client and the work we do for them. They seem to be typical racehorse breeders and trainers. He has put his flirting to the side for the moment.

The bluestone gates of the racing establishment, designed and built to impress, lead to a reception building, but we take the fork to the racing stables along a gravel driveway. This is the same place where Nerida dropped off the tubs this morning. Strange to double up on driving.

Michael introduces me to Alan, the training manager, and his staff as the newest and most attractive addition to the vet clinic. According to Michael, new blood ensures that the male staff stay motivated and don't look for work elsewhere.

Alan laughs and shakes my hand.

"Just ignore him, Riona. He's all bluff. All growl and no bite. Or, as my brother says, all hat and no cattle."

If only he knew, I think to myself, giving Alan a friendly smile. They have a well-oiled routine between themselves and Michael. I'm not required for anything. At the end of the call, Michael hands me the rack of blood tubes and a sheet of paper with the names of the racehorses matching those on the blood tubes.

"Make sure you don't drop them; otherwise, we'll need to do it again."

Alan rolls his eyes and laughs.

"She doesn't look stupid, Michael."

On the way back, we bypass the town with the super-market, but I don't dare to ask for a stop. Precious will have to wait for cat food.

I am not keen on small talk with Michael and search for something to say.

"Nice car, this Raptor," I begin the conversation.

"It's not a car; it's a truck," he says and spends about ten minutes describing all of its bells and whistles. He says he goes hunting for wild pigs sometimes. I don't believe a word he says except that the purchase price of the car was over $300,000.

"Wow, I didn't know you made enough money here to afford that kind of car. Truck, I mean, sorry."

He ignores my comment, and that signals the end of that conversation.

"What are the neighbors like?" I ask, leaving open the finer details of whether I mean neighbors close to the cottage or the vet clinic in general.

"The neighbors? There aren't many. Next to the cottage is only one. I'm surprised he hasn't turned up yet with some complaint or demand, the clown."

"What's he like?"

"You'll find out soon. I recommend not having a dog, though. He will shoot yours if it gets on his place."

"Great, two unsavory males in my life now," I say.

"Knock it off! No need to get personal."

As he parks the Raptor at the clinic, he grabs the rack of blood tubes and the sheet of paper from my hand.

"Home time, Riona. For you, at least. I'll run the bloods and do the paperwork before I go home."

I don't ask where he lives because he could construe that as interest.

Chapter 7

I turn on my music player. The music of the movie Babe calms my still jittery nerves.

Glad my first day went by without a hitch, I realize I am completely superfluous in this place. There's something strange going on here that I can't put my finger on. Too many staff, not enough clients. What is going on?

I muck out Princess' yard and slip her halter and rope on.

"Come on, time for a little nibble of herbs and grasses around the garden bed, Princess. Maybe we'll find some useful plants under all the weeds."

I love watching her snatching small mouthfuls and carefully selecting her preferred morsels. She wouldn't even need a lead rope because she follows me like a trained dog, but this is a strange place for her, and she might spook.

This is the best part of today. Life with my horse—how I have missed it during rehab. Even though I am not game enough yet to ride her, I imagine myself on her back.

"Let's see whether the fence is sound around this paddock. You might be lucky and have your own paddock for three months."

We wander along the fence, checking for holes, broken wires, and wires on the ground, but we find everything is in perfect order. On the other side of the fence, sheep scatter as we approach.

This must be the neighbor's property. It looks neat and not overstocked. Admirable, even if he shoots other people's dogs.

Just before I'm ready to turn back, a Nissan pickup roars up the paddock toward where we stand.

"There you go, Princess. Our neighbor, the clown. I think he's a nosy neighbor."

As he has obviously spotted me and Princess already, there is no point in leaving. That would be rude, and I don't want to be rude at first sight.

George wags his tail in anticipation of meeting new friends. I tell him to sit.

The Nissan turns in a circle, nose back to where it came from, and the driver gets out slower than I thought he would. On the back tray are three dogs, two red Kelpies, and a black-and-white Border Collie. They watch him silently, probably hoping they will be let off their chains.

He looks older than what Mum would call 'a young bloke' but younger than middle-aged, thin without looking too scrawny, and tall but appearing smaller because of his slouching shoulders. A man who doesn't want to stand out or a man comfortable within himself who doesn't care what others think of him?

"Hi, glad to meet you," he says, stretching out his rough hand across the fence. He looks at Princess and, with a slightly lop-sided grin that doesn't show his teeth, focuses his gray eyes on my face. The blood rushes to my face; annoying, but there's nothing I can do about it. The gray eyes remind me of Alaska, where I went with Mum and Dad on one of Dad's fishing adventures.

His eyes are darker than those of a Malamute dog but lighter than a wolf's, bright and with a dark ring between the iris and the white of his eyes. Fascinating, intense, slightly disturbing, but also calming my heartbeat after the initial rush.

He seems to notice that I'm disturbed by his gaze and looks away.

"Nice horse you got there," he says. "I'm Rocky McKillop, your neighbor. When did you move in?"

He doesn't wait for an answer. "I guess you must be their new intern or locum or whatever they call the likes of you."

"Intern. My name is Riona Clay. I moved in yesterday and will be here for three months, I think."

"Sick of it already?" Rocky laughs. I like his laugh.

"No, not at all, but there doesn't seem to be much work here."

"Give it some time. If you get bored, you can always come over for some sheep or cattle work if you like."

"I'm sure they will find something for me to do."

"Just in case you need help with something, I'll give you my phone number. Especially if it relates to anything fire, I am the man. I am the chief of the local fire brigade."

Rocky walks to his Nissan and writes down his phone number on a piece of paper that has probably been in his car for a few years. His Blundstones are old, and the bottoms of his jeans are slightly frayed.

He hands the snippet of an old invoice with his phone number scrawled on it to me and points his right index finger to the brim of his misshapen farm hat. I can't see the color of his hair in the afternoon light, but I think it might be blond, maybe gray, but probably not too gray.

"Cheers, see you later." His dogs stop wagging their tails, knowing their expected workout will not happen.

Rocky's Nissan crawls its way off toward a stand of gum trees that conceals his farmhouse.

I put the paper in my pocket even though I have already memorized the number. That is the only advantage I gained from my accident. Since I woke up from my coma, I can memorize anything new easily, but I can't remember some things from my past.

He ignores George, so I assume he doesn't mind my Kelpie, considering he has two of his own. Princess follows me to her stable for a scoop of horse pellets.

"Good night," I say, stroking the half-moon scar on her forehead."

I take the twitch off my belt and place it on the kitchen table, right next to my phone and the car keys, ready for tomorrow morning. Ready to prepare dinner for myself.

With two eggs, a couple of ripe tomatoes, and a big T-bone steak out of the fridge, there will be a feast in honor of my first day at work. I'm ready to cook dinner and call Mum.

Mum had packed a bag of carrots and potatoes so that I wouldn't starve. There are also stock cubes, onions, and garlic—plenty to throw together a dinner for one.

While I busy myself with the ingredients, I think about Rocky. He didn't seem a bad sort. Mum would say he would scrub up nicely if put into city clothes instead of his oversized checkered shirt, ripped jeans, farm boots, and the weird farm hat.

I keep imagining his gray eyes. I have never seen a man with eyes like that. He probably kept looking at me in his rearview mirror on his way home. What did he see in me? He seemed intense, trying to appear calm and neutral. At least he makes a better neighbor than Michael. Unless he comes here to shoot George.

I put on music for myself. Chariots of Fire seems a good choice for a steak dinner. I dance around the kitchen table, matching its beat.

The door to the cabinet behind the paneling is slightly open. The cat made herself comfortable on the lowest book shelf and gives me a two-eyed blink before burying her nose back in her tail.

Chapter 8

The knob of butter is sizzling, and I'm ready to put the steak into the griddle pan when a rumble outside the front door reminds George that he is a watchdog. He jumps up from under the table and darts to the front door, barking as if he were ready to rip the approaching intruder apart.

"Who can that be? Rocky?" The blood drains from my face toward my heart when I open the door.

"Dadah! It's only me, Riona," says Michael cheerfully, sticking his car keys into the back pocket of his designer denim shorts and holding a bottle of red wine out toward me.

This means he wants to stay—at least for a while. "No need to be worried."

"What do you want? Is there an emergency?"

"Oh no, there is no emergency. I just bought a nice bottle of red at the supermarket. Just for you! Won't you let me in? I can smell dinner. It is always better to have dinner for two than for one, don't you think?"

"No, I don't think that at all. But by all means, tell me why you are here." I didn't say, 'Come in,' but he barges past me into the living room.

"I better switch the griddle pan off, so I don't have charcoal for dinner," my hint that dinner for two is off the table.

Michael plonks himself down on the sofa opposite the fireplace, the hundred-year-old piece of furniture sagging under his weight. He spreads his arms along the backrest as if he owns the place. I sit down in one of the armchairs beside the fireplace, George next to me on the carpet, facing Michael. As if from nowhere, Precious appears and jumps up on the armrest of my chair, arranging her body into the ancient Egyptian statue shape of our first acquaintance.

My raised eyebrows should hint to Michael that I am waiting impatiently for a logical explanation for his visit.

"I just thought I would explain this place to you," he says.

"What is there to explain? It's all well set up, all the electricity and the plumbing works. It's still too warm to put the fireplace on; otherwise, nothing tells me this is inferior accommodation. I have seen worse."

"That may be so, but this place has a few quirks."

"There are only two comments to that. One, how do you know there are quirks? And Two, why would these quirks need explaining?"

"As to One, I lived here as an intern and found out that this cottage is not as ordinary as it seems."

"To me, it looks quite an ordinary cottage," I dismiss his explanation. "Old and tired, but functional."

"Just take note of your demon cat. She is no ordinary cat at all. She is evil."

Precious opens her mouth for the biggest yawn I'd ever seen, curling up her pink tongue and showing off her pristine teeth. She shuts her mouth and gives Michael a dark stare, unblinking, with pupils round and black.

I laugh, which seems to raise Michael's anger.

"See what I mean. Look at her face! Pure evil."

"Leave my cat alone," I say. "So, what about Two? What is so bad that you have to make a special visit to warn me about it?

"That cat is not the only thing. I agree she might be fine with you. She might be even just like you, an evil witch."

I laugh again. "What other things are there that bothered you with this cottage?"

"That portrait over the fireplace, for example."

"What is wrong with it?"

"Can't you see? Come over here, and you can see it!"

I walk over to the sofa and stand next to Michael, studying the painting.

It is the same lady as at lunchtime. She hasn't changed.

"I can't see anything wrong with her."

"You can't? Can't you see her evil smirk? She has a condescending smirk on her face. She looks like a real man hater."

"Oh, get over it. She does not have a smirk. How can you get so out of tune just because of a cat and a painting? Anything else?"

"You'll find out—sooner or later. But if not, then be glad. I couldn't get out of here soon enough."

I feel sorry for Michael now, wondering how anything could fool him or cause him to be superstitious or scared.

I walk back into the kitchen, leaving him behind on the sofa, to switch the griddle pan on again. I realize I have lost all fear of him after this short conversation. I'll throw him out when the steak is done.

I grease the pan with a second generous nob of butter.

"Hey, Michael, can you please explain one thing to me? Why aren't there any horses in the hospital? I asked you before, but your answer was a bit vague. What is the reason? Five fully experienced vets, plus me, don't seem to have much to do. Why do you need an intern? I felt totally superfluous today."

There is a pause in the living room, and then Michael appears in the kitchen doorway.

"No particular reason. There will be work and sometimes there is more work than we can handle. You'll find out soon enough."

"Yes, otherwise, I'm just the newbie vet with the twitch.'

"More like the witch with the twitch," says Michael. "In the meantime, you better keep your nosy nose out of things that don't concern you. That is the only tip I can give you."

"Oh, is there anything specific that I should not be nosy about?"

He walks around the kitchen table toward me, smiling and pulling his bushy blond eyebrows up. A deep V-shaped furrow appears on his forehead. As I turn toward the table to put the steak in the griddle pan, he reaches over to me with one hand while planting the other one on the tabletop.

"Don't be such a smartie-pants prude," he grabs my waist and pulls me toward him. "It's better to have me as a friend than an enemy."

"Michael, just leave it. You better go home now. Let me go!"

He squeezes my waist harder. I freeze, imagining him with the black stripes of the hot griddle pan engraved on his face or slapping him with the raw steak. I could also squash one of these deliciously ripe tomatoes right in the middle of his nose. The hot griddle pan is tempting but I pick up the steak.

Michael laughs as if he has read my mind.

"Let me go," I say, still holding the steak. Somehow, George misunderstood. He heard the word go and thought I held the steak up for him to catch. He jumps at the steak, I lift it higher, and George tries to grab it with his teeth, bumping into my uninvited visitor.

Michael flinches and steps back, knocking the eggs off the table. Somehow, in the commotion, the twitch rolls off the table, too. He slips on the raw egg and loses his footing, trying to avoid the dog or a slap with the steak. He lands on the kitchen floor with his thigh on the twitch and the steak on his shoulder.

I can't help but laugh at this picture.

"Ouch," screams Michael as I quietly pick up the steak from his shoulder and place it in the sizzling butter in the pan.

"Sorry, Michael, I need the steak."

I feel comforted by the sizzle in the pan and assured that the pain in his gym-enhanced thigh will be enough to stop him from becoming too friendly again.

George barks like crazy at Michael. I wonder if he is angry to have lost the steak.

"You are a witch," says Michael and gathers himself up from the kitchen floorboards, shaking the raw egg slime from his hands.

"It's made of mahogany," I say.

"What's made of mahogany?"

"The twitch. I got it from my grandmother."

"She was probably a witch too, just like you."

"Maybe," I say, waving my hands before his face. "Wooohooohoo! Watch the bats and vampires on your way home."

He scurries out the front door, rubbing his thigh, but has the presence of mind to grab the bottle of wine from the table on the way out. I call George, who obediently flops himself on the carpet in the living room, his mouth open in a big grin after all the barking.

The Raptor roars off, spitting gravel at my front door. I slam it shut with my foot.

"Good riddance," I say to Precious as she blinks at me twice from the armrest.

"Time to have dinner, children," I say while steadying my wobbly knees.

The steak is a little overdone, but I don't mind.

Chapter 9

"*Wake up! Riona, wake up!*"
"*Yes, Nan, I will.*"

I'm dreaming that I'm still in a coma, immobile in bed, comfortable and without pain. Nan is telling me to wake up.

"Yes, Nan, I am awake," I say and sit up in a jolt. It is pitch dark.

I hear Princess galloping around her yard, neighing, and George barking non-stop in his kennel.

I can't find the switch for the porch light?

Never mind, the phone light will have to do. I let George out of his kennel. Better to have a protector with me, but he clings to my legs, wanting protection from me.

"What's wrong, Princess?" I call out as I walk over to her yard barefoot.

The horse calms down a little when she sees and hears me, but she keeps looking in the direction of the clinic, head held high, and ears pricked. She snorts in anger and to warn, not once, but several times. I listen for answers from other horses, but I hear nothing. The night is silent.

"It is all fine, Princess. Look. George is fine, too. Maybe some kangaroos moved through. You don't know kangaroos, I think. Don't worry, you'll get used to them."

I pat Princess' sweaty neck and face and stay with her until she puts her head down to the ground to give her food bowl a shove.

"Come on, George. Entertainment is over. Back inside."

He follows me and hops on my bed to make sure I don't put him in the kennel again. I don't tell him off, and after a while, we nod off.

PING

The screen of my phone tells me I have a message. Michael! What does he want now?

'Surgery tomorrow morning at 8:30. Be here by 8:00 to help set up and assist with anesthesia.'

It is four o'clock. My alarm is already set for 6:30, so I wouldn't be late even without the reminder. Why did he send this text to me at this time of the night? To annoy me and interrupt my sleep, I suppose.

Why did I hear Nan talking? She died almost a year ago, on the day of my accident. I heard her all the time calling my name, trying to wake me up from my coma. I wish I could have said goodbye to her, but it was not to be. I never told Mum that Nan talked to me in my coma because I knew she would never believe me.

But what about now? I'm no longer in a coma. I dreamed I was back in the hospital, and she called me. I try to recall my dream and realize I didn't dream of being in a coma. I just heard her call me. What if she really did?

Is this one of the creepy things Michael tried to tell me that happens in this house? But I wouldn't call Nan talking to me creepy, even if I thought she spoke to me from the other side to wake me up from my coma.

I must have nodded off again eventually because the alarm catches me by surprise. I jump into the shower and pull a clean blue t-shirt over me before putting on my newest pair of jeans for this special day, my first surgery. At least something is happening now.

Feeding Princess and George leaves me barely enough time to scoff down some muesli with yogurt before I grab the twitch and clip it to my belt.

With every step along the brick path, my confidence evaporates a little more. What if I can't do it?

I have never prepared any surgery kit, let alone an entire operating theatre. I feel so out of depth, not remotely ready to assist yet in surgery. Will I be able to work out how the anesthetic machine works? I wish I had read the user manual, at least.

"I hope someone will be there to teach me how to prepare the horse for its operation," I mumble.

"The nurses must be able to help me put the right instruments together. I wonder who is going to do the surgery, Leonard or Michael. Leonard, probably because Michael is only two years ahead of me in knowledge and skills."

I still wonder what spooked Princess and George. Maybe someone brought the horse with its injury in during the night. But I should have heard that. The gate wouldn't have opened without the intercom telling me to open it.

"Never mind, all will be revealed," I whisper as I walk along the brick path to the hospital building.

"What the ... ?"

The carpark is full of vehicles that have nothing to do with horses or a vet clinic. There are two ambulances, which freaks me out, and several police cars, some with their lights flashing even though they are parked. Unmarked cars are among them. Michael's Raptor is in the same spot as yesterday. Amy's car and a couple of vet cars with the clinic logo on their doors are parked next to it.

I sprint to the entry of the stable breezeway and am immediately blocked by blue and white police tape.

Amy is standing inside, dabbing her eyes with tissue, talking to a man in a dark blue suit who looks like the conductor of my high school's symphony orchestra. His wild red hair is tied at the back into a ponytail, and his much darker full beard looks so out of place in the breezeway.

"Amy, what's going on?" I call out to her.

"Michael is dead," she sobs.

"What? Did he get kicked by a horse?"

The man gently shoos Amy out under the crime scene tape.

"No, he just died, or he killed himself," she sobs, snorting into her tissue.

"What? But he was alright yesterday. He was perfectly fine and his usual self. This is crazy. When did it happen?"

"Sometime during the night, they say."

"How did it happen, Amy?"

"They found him in the operating theatre on the operating table, attached to the anesthetic machine."

"No way, Amy. How is that possible?"

I brush under the tape and walk past the recovery stall and the set of three freezers to the double doors of the operating theatre.

"You can't come in here," says a stern voice that belongs to the man with the wild hair. He grabs me by the arm and pulls me away so I can't get a glimpse inside the fully lit room.

"And who might you be? Why are you so keenly interested in what's going on here?"

"I am one of the vets here, Riona ...." My voice trails off as I see the ambos come out, pulling a stretcher with a covered body on it. I can't think straight. Yesterday, I could have wished all kinds of horrible accidents to befall Michael, but not death. The body under the covers doesn't make any sense to me.

I feel my vision blur and the world spin. If I don't want to land head-first on the concrete, passing out, I need to sit down on the floor.

"I'm sorry, I feel nauseous."

The black shoes of the man in the dark blue suit slowly come into focus.

"I am Chief Inspector Brown. Are you all right? Constable Nadia will get you some water. But I will have some questions for you later if you don't mind."

He walks off, leaving me where I sit without waiting for an answer. He's a man showing he is in charge of everything.

From my low vantage point, I watch people going in and out of the operating theatre, carrying boxes and evidence bags. Photographers are taking photos of the fancy new anesthetic machine, which must have cost tens of thousands of dollars and now has become a focus of suspicion.

Leonard is busy explaining how the machine works, and after a while, a forensic team covers and tapes the machine up with plastic sheets.

There goes our most important surgery tool. There will be no more surgeries until they are finished examining it for clues, which could take a while.

"This will take a while," says Inspector Brown to me as if he has read my mind. "I hear you live on the property?"

I nod.

"I need nothing from you right now except when and where you saw Michael last.

"I saw him yesterday evening after work, around 8 o'clock, when he visited me in the cottage. He left about half an hour later, but I don't know where he went. He must have come here because his Raptor is here."

"So, did you see him anytime during the night, or did he call you? Or maybe you called him?"

"No, negative on all questions. But he texted me at 4am to ask me to assist this morning with surgery."

"Interesting. I suggest you go back to your cottage and stay there until we finish here. I don't want to hold up this business for longer than I have to. When I am done here, I'll meet you at your cottage."

He turns without further comment, leaving me to wait a few more minutes to get up. Apart from the police vehicles and the Raptor, the car park is now empty. The red bricks of the path to the cottage radiate the midday heat through the soles of my boots.

Chapter 10

I let George out of his dog run to roam free before I sit down on the lone chair in front of Princess' stable. She comes over for a pat but then leaves again. Precious appears from under a bush, tail held high, and rubs against my leg.

What a crazy day. I want to call Mum, but she would tell me to pack up and come home.

I put the twitch on the kitchen table and flop into the armchair next to the fireplace.

Precious leaps on the armrest and rubs her head on my elbow, purr motor rumbling in her throat and her amber eyes trying to soothe my soul. I feel so lonely and out of place.

"Oh, Nan, I wish you were here to talk to about what happened today."

"Meeh," says Precious, as if she understood. But I hear Nan answer in my head.

"I am here, Love. We can talk any time you like."

I jump up like a rocket from a launchpad, the hair on the back of my neck rising out of the base of my ponytail. I realize the voice is not in my head.

But I also know Nan is not really in the room with me. It only sounds like she sits in the armchair on the other side of the fireplace.

"Get used to it, Riona; I am here, and we can solve this mystery together."

It dawns on me that Michael was right. This cottage is spooky. Or I've gone mad.

"But Nan, you're not real. I can't see you. How can you be real? There are no such things as ghosts. I am a scientist, and I don't do paranormal stuff. How can you talk to me and say you're here?"

"Hmmm. Darling, don't worry. There is more to reality than you think, but I won't spook you with the details, as your generation calls it. We'll talk about that later.

Am I going crazy? It wouldn't surprise me, considering that my brain was out of action and operated on by neurosurgeons to keep it from decomposing in my head after my crash. But even though I feel fragile sometimes and easily stressed, I had hoped this new job would help me steady my life without becoming a weirdo and a curiosity for others.

"You won't remember this, but when you were in your coma, we passed each other. I was on my way to the other side, and you couldn't decide which way you were going, to the other side or back into the real world. We passed each other on that day, and some of our energy must have gotten mixed up at that moment. I didn't pass all the way over, and now I'm in a kind of Limbo. Never mind, you will learn to recognize my presence."

I don't dare to interrupt her and can only muster a whispered "Why, Nan?"

"There are several reasons why I couldn't pass yet. The main one is probably that I have unfinished business here with this place; otherwise, you wouldn't have ended up here."

"What does that mean, Nan, our energy getting mixed up? And what do I have to do with this place here?"

"You will work it out, dear, trust me. At this moment, you need to focus on what happened here yesterday."

"I don't know what happened here. I don't think anything happened here at all. I didn't hear or see anything unusual."

"I woke you up to take notice in the middle of the night, don't you remember?"

Precious digs her claws into my thigh, kneading furiously. Does this mean she agrees with my invisible Nan?

I get up from the chair to make myself a pot of tea. Making tea is always a good time waster for steadying my nerves.

"I do remember, Nan."

While the kettle boils, I open up Notes on my phone.

What do I know? And why did Nan wake me up in the middle of the night? I jot my thoughts down.

Something spooked Princess and George. What did they hear? I remember hearing nothing, no horse, no dog, no car. Nothing. The gate did not alert me through the intercom that someone was waiting to come into the car park. When exactly was that? I can't remember.

"It was exactly five minutes before midnight," says Nan. "I was here with you, so I don't know what happened over at the hospital at that time. I am clueless, like you."

Whatever spooked my animals stopped being spooky about half an hour after they started their racket.

What happened then?

Nothing. So I went to bed until I got a text from Michael; at 4am.

Texting your coworker at 4am is not a normal thing to do.

"There you go," says invisible Nan. "You got your first clue."

"Why was Michael up at that time?"

"These are all clues, Riona."

I wonder whether there was a real horse booked in for surgery. Maybe Michael made that all up. If there had been a horse coming in during the night, the owners would have activated the gate intercom. One advantage of my coma was that I now have a better memory for clues like numbers and small details that others might never recall.

"I'll get on it, Nan. I just wonder if anyone else heard anything during the night. Maybe the neighbor heard something."

"I think you should wait until the police have finished their work today. They might turn up with more questions before the day is out. They might give you a hint or two that you can use."

I nod, even though I know she can't see me.

"Why don't you have a look through the green trunk in the meantime? You may find a few things that might help you improve your skills."

"What do you mean, Nan?".

She does not answer. I delete all my notes because they don't seem helpful. I can't say I feel calmer now that I can talk to her. I always had a special connection with Nan, but why did she have to go that far and contact me now from the other side? Does this mean I can talk to ghosts?

Chapter 11

I tidy away the contents of the three remaining boxes of my possessions into the bedroom cupboard and move the old lady from her hook into the spare bedroom, where she can supervise what appears to be an old herb garden next to the dog kennel.

I pour myself another cup of tea, my hands still jittery, and unlock the green trunk again. Now is as good a time as any to sort through the stuff. Maybe Nan appearing as a ghost gives me a little more motivation to find out what she has left me. Some of it might be useful as living room decorations and bookshelf fillers.

Yesterday, I ignored the 'Paranormal Monthly'. Let's start with it now.

The magazine is from last year. Last year, just before she died? I still can't get over Nan reading this type of publication in her old age. But considering she's revealed herself as a ghost now, it seems more normal than paranormal.

I smile to myself, turning the pages.

There is an article about a woman named Eileen Anderson. I know Nan was born an Anderson. Is this why she was interested in the article? Or why she wants me to look in this trunk now?

But what shakes me more than Nan's interest in weird ideas, is the picture at the top of the article. I hold it up to compare it to the painting above the fireplace, the one that Michael found spooky and evil.

It is definitely the same woman; different dress, but the necklace is the same. I am totally confused. What the ....?

I put down the magazine after reading the article. The woman named Eileen in the article is my great-grandmother, and her daughter Ana, or Anastasia, is my grandmother, my Nan. The article claims they were witches. Two of my ancestors were supposed to be witches? What does that make me?

Why did Nan want me to read this article? Am I supposed to be a witch, too? I don't need a complicated life. It is complicated enough as it is. I don't want to be a witch. I want to be normal, like everyone else.

Precious weaves excitedly around my legs, purring with encouragement as I keep rummaging through the trunk.

In the elegant jewelry box, amongst gemstones that must be fake, is the exact necklace that Eileen is wearing in the painting above the fireplace. This means there is no coincidence. What is Nan telling me?

I lay out the small collection of framed pictures and photos on the sofa and then look for suitable picture hooks on the walls. The photos are old, making it hard to recognize who anyone is. Fortunately, Nan has written the names of the people in the pictures on the backs. I realize that Eileen's name was, in fact, Elena and that she has a sister, Swetlana, and a brother, Alexej. Why did Elena call herself Eileen?

There are pictures of Elena's mother, Friederike, and her father, Wladimir Woynewitch, in their Russian outfits from the turn of the century. I realize the old woman in the other painting is Friederike Woynewitch.

I am annoyed that Mum has never told me about my Russian Ancestors. I need to ask Nan about what Mum has not dared to tell me. I stack the pictures up to revisit with Nan once she makes herself known again.

There is a small gold-framed photo, an olden-day postcard of a little house. An electric jolt stings my heart. It's this cottage, the very cottage I live in, surrounded by trees much younger and smaller than the majestic redgums that are now almost fully grown decades later.

The only difference I can see is the front door. It has a patterned lead glass panel at the top, but I cannot decipher the pattern. With the picture in my hand, I rush to open the front door and discover that someone has nailed or screwed a piece of plywood over the outside of the glass window, which would have taken up the upper quarter of the door.

Disappointed, I shut it to inspect its inside surface. There is no plywood to cover the glass on the inside, but someone has glued a piece of brown packaging paper over it.

I need to get this paper off to see what it hides.

Armed with a large knife from the kitchen, I slice the paper at its lower edge. There is a gap underneath, and once I have peeled off the brittle brown paper, the details of the glass panel become visible, a colorful lead glass window of a pair of blue wrens on an ornate tree branch. I take a picture of it and then enlarge it to see what the lead letters in the picture say.

I flip it horizontally, as it was meant to be read from the outside.

Blue Wren Cottage, it says. Two birds sit on a branch with the words 'Blue Wren' above and 'Cottage' below them.

How cute, I think, but then I notice that one of the small colorful panes of the picture has a hole in it, with cracks radiating out from its center. A bullet hole?

I stare at what someone has carefully hidden from the world. The paper on the inside is so brittle that it must have been there for many decades. The outside plywood has been covered with the same dark green paint used for all the verandah posts, the window frames, and the rest of the door.

Why am I here? There can't be any coincidence that I ended up in this very cottage that Nan and her mother knew. But why now? What happened here?

I throw the old paper scraps into the rubbish bin in the kitchen and take a bunch of notebooks from the trunk. The books, with their drawings and descriptions of poisonous plants, may come in handy one day. I leaf through a notebook that is written in German. That must be one of Eileen's. I always wondered why Nan made me learn German and why she spoke it so fluently herself. The notes refer to common ailments of horses and how to treat them with medicines made from plants and minerals.

There is also the book of spells. On the cover, it says, 'With translation from Russian into English'. I don't understand why Nan has a Russian book on spells, but I am confident now that Nan saw herself as a practicing witch. The spells are written in a tidy Russian script with the translations in the pages' margins.

What do I do with these books now? I can't leave them lying around willy-nilly in the living room or on the bookshelves beside the fireplace. I don't want to be known for witchcraft. More importantly, if the police come to interview me here, books with poison plants and alternative medicines might not be something that would help me dispel their suspicions.

I decorate the otherwise empty bookshelves in the living room with the crystals, little glass jars, and beakers from the trunk. Placing the tiny golden sickle as an ornament on the mantlepiece under Elena's portrait cheers me up. It looks so shiny and bright.

I gather the books and the jewelry box and carry them to the small cabinet behind the wall paneling.

On the way out, I pass by the map again. Knowing that Nan and her mother must have lived here at some point, I try harder than I had yesterday to understand the layout of the property at the time the map was printed in 1920, just before Eileen arrived here.

Using my finger to trace the old fence lines, I discover the little block with the cottage was only a tiny speck on the map. It is marked *B W Cottage* and is at the end of Cottage Lane. Another lane, Green Bowlder Lane, leads from the east to the back fence of the cottage garden.

I wonder whether Green Bowlder Lane is still there. I'll have a look later when I put Princess into the grass field. It looks like this lane goes in the direction that Rocky came from with his three dogs yesterday. I cannot find a house on the map confirming someone lived there in 1920.

Startled by George barking, I shut the door to the small windowless room and lock the trunk. Before I even get to the front door to see who has arrived, there is a knock.

Chapter 12

"Good afternoon, Mr. Brown."

He walks past me into the living room, light-footed in his black shoes.

I stand aside, leaving the front door wide open to disguise the fact I ripped off the paper on the inside of the glass panel. A door with a bullet hole might not be the best start to a police interview.

"It's Chief Inspector, not Mr. Brown. I see you have settled in already."

"I don't have many possessions to get settled in with, but I'm getting there. The cottage is set up well, and I don't need much. Would you like to have a cup of tea? Or a cup of coffee? I have a great French Press to make you a coffee you won't forget."

"No, thank you. I just want to clear up a couple of things."

"Like what?" I ask, a little reluctantly, now that I know my family had some connection to this place in the past and that I have a front door with a bullet hole. It might complicate the whole situation.

Chief Inspector Brown sits down in the exact spot where Michael had sat, scanning the room. I sit down opposite on my usual chair next to the fireplace, wondering whether Nan is somewhere close by, watching from her ghostly side of the universe.

"Tell me again, why your colleague came to visit yesterday."

"I don't really know why he came except to tell me that the cat is evil and the cottage is spooky. He wanted to stay for dinner, but I told him to leave. He was irritating, trying to gossip about anyone and everything around here."

"Interesting. Why didn't you want him to stay for dinner? Isn't it a little rude to turn one of your coworkers down when they come to check on you after your first day at work?"

"It was more like checking up on me to see if he could hook up with me, I think."

"I see. What gave you that impression?"

"Nothing in particular, except ... " I catch myself in time from saying that that was Michael's MO.

"Except that you knew him from university."

"That was a long time ago. We both started at the same time in our vet courses some years ago. I took a gap year in Europe after my first year, and I haven't seen him since then."

"And how was he then compared to now? Or vice versa."

"I don't think he changed much. He was always very impressed with himself and his effect on women."

"So, you say he was a womanizer?"

"No, I didn't say that. He was very popular with most of the girls five years ago, but I don't know whether that was still the case here and now."

"What was your relationship with him when you met him again here?"

"There was no relationship. He took me on an outside call to a racing stable yesterday afternoon. We only talked about his car, the imported three-hundred-thousand-dollar marvel of a Raptor, and that I should keep my nose out of anything to do with the vet hospital."

"What things in particular?"

"That I don't know."

His furrowed eyebrows tell me that he doesn't believe me.

"I think I'll make a pot of tea," I say calmly as if I hadn't noticed. The detective follows me into the kitchen. "I'll make one for you too. Milk? Sugar?" He is taller than me and smells of an expensive aftershave.

"Just milk, please."

"So, what happened to Michael? How did he die?" I choose a big mug with a horse picture for him, to give him the impression I am not worried about a long interview.

"We don't know yet. We have to wait for the post-mortem."

He picks up the twitch and weighs it in his hand like a police truncheon of old. He then twirls and waves it about in front of his head.

"You look like the conductor of our school orchestra with his baton," I giggle.

"What is this thing?"

"This is a twitch to subdue unruly horses. It's a very handy tool."

"I see. Could it be used to subdue a person?"

"I can't imagine someone would even try that. No. I don't think so.

"You said Michael was gossiping. What did he gossip about?" The detective examines the carved surface of the mahogany handle.

"Only that the neighbor was a nasty clown and would shoot my dog, but I don't think that's true. I met him over the fence, and he didn't seem like an unhinged guy who would shoot animals. He seemed like a normal farmer to me, plus he's the chief of the local fire brigade."

"This looks like old wood."

"Yes, it is quite ancient, I believe. I think it is from 1870, as you can see from the carved number on the handle. It was a present from my grandmother."

"Now, is there anything unusual that you have noticed around here, considering that Michael told you to keep your nose out of things? Is there anything else that caught your eye or ear?"

"The only thing unusual was that I woke up just before midnight because the dog barked like crazy, and the horse was unsettled in the yard. And that Michael sent me a text to say a horse was coming in for surgery in the morning, and I should be there to assist."

"Any reason why the dog barked?"

"No, I couldn't hear or see anything at all. They calmed down after maybe twenty minutes.

The detective put the twitch on the table, carefully as if it could break.

"Can I have a quick look through your house and your car, if you don't mind?"

"No problem at all."

I walk ahead of him, followed by George and the cat, as he looks into each room and then walks out to the car.

Chief Inspector Brown opens all the doors one by one, having a look around, and then into the back. He seems satisfied I haven't stored any murder weapon there. Before getting into his unmarked car, he turns around again.

"So, your dog-shooting neighbor lives down that way?"

"Yes." I point toward his farm, past Princess, who stands, like a statue, at the fence watching us.

"Nice horse you've got there."

"Yes, I know. I am very blessed with my animals."

He laughs his quiet little laugh and starts the car.

"I'd appreciate it if you could stay put on this property here until we have sorted when and how the deceased died. When did you say you received his message after he left?"

"I didn't say, but it was at 4am. Not a time to send messages to coworkers, in my opinion. And there was no horse in the morning that needed surgery. So, it was all fake, I think."

Chapter 13

I wait at the door until I am sure Chief Inspector Brown has left for good and then push the trunk in front of the hidden door. I might place a nice rock from the paddock on it to give the green metal box a purely ornamental appearance.

My stomach reminds me I forgot to eat lunch, but it's late afternoon by now, and I think it's time to take Princess for a walk instead of messing up my eating routine.

I slip the halter over her head and lead her out into the small paddock. Walking in an easterly direction, I wonder if I can find Green Bowlder Lane. The grass is long and has begun to hay off. After fifty meters or so, I hit the fence line, but I don't find anything resembling a lane. Maybe someone has ripped out the garden and any fruit trees that might have been planted to make way for the little paddock that Princess seems to enjoy.

Disappointed, I'm about to turn back as I see Rocky's familiar Nissan pickup creeping up to the fence. Maybe he knows something about Green Bowlder Lane. I wait, one foot on the lowest fence wire, leaning on Princess' shoulder and stroking her mane.

"Long time no see," he says after parking the pickup a few meters from the fence. His dogs are wagging their tails at George and jump off the truck to greet him through the fence.

"You could say that. Lots of things happened here since we met last."

"I heard. One shouldn't speak ill of the dead, but it couldn't have happened to a nicer guy."

I don't quite know how to respond to that comment, but his face tells me it wasn't meant as a joke.

"Why do you say that? He did mention to me that you two had your differences."

"Not differences personally. Just differences about how to manage the vegetation around the cottage here and on the hospital premises."

"I see, but wouldn't that be Leonard's business and not Michael's?" I say without understanding.

"He lived in the cottage last year and didn't mow the grass once, nor had it grazed down. I offered him some sheep to do the job of fire prevention. But he accused me of trying to get free grazing for my sheep. Leonard backed him up, and so we didn't end up being friendly neighbors. We stayed out of each other's way."

"But that's no reason to wish him dead."

"No, I didn't wish him dead, but that wasn't all. His German Shepherd came out one night, ganged up with Leonard's two Jack Russell terriers, and the three of them hunted my sheep."

"Oh, no! That's terrible."

"I told him I would shoot the dogs if they came back and were caught on my property again. I think Michael gave the dog away because I never saw him again, but they never apologized."

"Did you hear anything going on last night? The police were here asking whether I saw or heard anything, but apart from something spooking my dog and horse halfway through the night, I didn't hear anything."

"My house is too far down from the hospital to hear anything if the wind doesn't come from the right direction. That's why I never heard the dogs hunting the sheep that night. Otherwise, I would have stopped it."

I could feel Rocky's anger and frustration with his neighbor and then remembered what I had come to the fence for in the first place.

"Rocky, I wonder about something. In the cottage, there is a map from 1920 that says there is a Green Bowlder Lane that leads from the cottage toward the East. That must be in your direction. Have you got any idea if that still exists or why it doesn't exist anymore? At least I can't find it, even though it is on the map in the cottage."

Rocky turns his head in the direction he'd come from and scratches his chin.

"I only have the fire brigade maps that we use and the normal maps that you can Google for directions. But there is a Green Bowlder Lane. Our farm is at 2 Green Bowlder Lane. We are right at the beginning of it near the road to town, but it ends not far from the home paddock. I think this was once all one station that was cut up some time ago. I can ask my grandfather about it. He should remember the why and when of it all."

"That would be super, Rocky," I say, fascinated by the concentration in his gray eyes.

"How about tomorrow here at the same time?" he suggests, slight crow's feet appearing when he smiles. "Sounds like a date, doesn't it?"

"It sure does," I burst out laughing. "With a wire fence in between us." My heart misses a beat, and the idea of a stormy autumn sky crosses my mind

He whistles after his three dogs, who were sniffing around on their side of the fence. They jump like rockets onto the bed of the pickup, their collar tags rattling and toe nails clicking on the metal. In a flash, George roars up to the fence and leaps over it. He cannot resist the whistle and jumps into the back of Rocky's pickup, joining his dogs, who don't seem to mind another companion.

Hey, you can't leave without me. I am a professional muster dog, he seems to say, a broad grin on his face and tongue flapping.

"Wait!" I yell after Rocky, who keeps driving toward his home, oblivious to the addition of another volunteer worker to his team of dogs.

"Never mind. He'll bring him back," I say to Princess, who resumes her grass picking. "I can understand why he didn't like Michael. "

While I am mucking out Princess' yard, I think about George. Maybe he misses working with sheep. He was Dad's muster dog, after all, busy with Dad every day before we moved to town because of my accident. Now, he is bored in his dog run while I am at work. I think Dad gave him to me for protection. Any dog is better than no dog for a single girl, he said. George isn't young anymore and would have to retire in a couple of years, anyway. I admit that I would feel lonely if I didn't have him with me, even though I have a cat now. I think the cat lets me believe I own her.

It doesn't take long, and the surprisingly meek beep-beep of Rocky's pickup sounds from the other side of the paddock. He lifts George off the back of the truck and drops him over the fence. I wave at him, and he points his hand to the brim of his hat before roaring back home.

George gallops up to me, greeting me with enthusiasm, as if he hadn't seen me for days.

"You are a traitor, bad boy," I say to him. "Let's have dinner. I wonder what will happen tomorrow."

As if my question had reverberated through the universe, a few minutes later, I receive an answer via text from Leonard.

'The police investigation at our hospital has been completed. We are allowed to resume our activities, and from tomorrow morning, it will be business as usual. I will be on call tonight. I expect everyone here at 8:00 am for a brief staff meeting. We will be extra busy tomorrow as people will come in just for curiosity.'

Chapter 14

Horse floats line up in the parking area, and horse owners lead their horses in small circles around until they are called to present them for examination.

I dread the staff meeting. Apart from Leonard and Lei, all staff are women. I wonder who will be grieving for Michael, who will be pretend-grieving. Who doesn't care, and who is overjoyed but not showing it? What questions do they have, and will they dare to ask them?

"Listen up, I want you to forget all about Michael now and think about your work today. People will ask questions to satisfy their curiosity and feed the gossip pipeline. Your answer should always be that you know nothing about anything. You were not here when it happened, so you have no clue. If they have questions, tell them they should ask the police."

We all nod silently, agreeing while eying each other suspiciously. Who is the killer amongst us? Who can we trust from now on?

"And you must fully bill them for every minute of the time they waste today with their supposedly sick horses.

However, make sure that the cases are worked up properly so you don't miss any real illness or condition."

We nod again.

"I have set up a new roster. This means that Riona will, from today, be one of the full-dutye vets, at least for the next three months, or until we can find a suitably qualified replacement for Michael."

My heart flutters in my chest. That means I need to get familiar with the main clients who might call in for services on a regular basis. How can I cover up my lack of practical experience? Certainly not with any witchcraft. That thought makes me smile, but not for long.

"I expect you to support each other and especially Riona, who is not familiar with the locations and roads around here. She may need to ask you questions during the day if she gets stuck with a case."

Everyone nods again, but I can see that Nerida pulls down the corners of her mouth as if answering a question of mine would be a complete imposition on her. I give her my most friendly smile and get a blank stare in return.

On the way out of the staffroom, I follow Amy to reception.

"Hey, Amy, I wonder whether you can give me a quick rundown on what you need from me when I do a call outside or a case in here."

"Come with me," she says. We spend about thirty minutes on how the billing and treatments work until I feel almost ready for my first 'real' day of work.

Phone calls interrupt my instruction a few times. One of the incoming calls is from the training stables that Michael and I visited to take blood. They are wondering where the results are. They had been expecting them last night. Amy promises to check on it.

"I'll check," I say to Amy. "I remember Michael said he'd run the blood tubes in the afternoon and would send them the results in the evening. He should have done that. I'll go find the results. Back in a minute."

The lab is deserted as everyone is outside with clients and horses. I am surprised to see the rack of blood tubes still on the bench. Had they been processed in the blood analyzer? I can't find the original sheets with the horses' names on them or the results sheet.

I don't understand. Michael said he was going back to the hospital to do that after he left my cottage.

Had he not gone back, or had he been killed before he could get the bloods done? There would have been plenty of time before four in the morning when he texted me. Or had they been analyzed, and the results disappeared somehow?

"Amy, Michael didn't get the blood results before he died. There are no results sheets anywhere."

"Really? But there was enough time to get the results before he went home after work. He didn't have far to go. He lives in the mansion and could have given them the results before the day was out."

"I didn't know he lived in the mansion. How strange. Can you ask Alan if he wants me to come back and take them again? I am happy to do that. Tell them we won't charge them for the extra time."

The morning went by in a blur, and then Amy asked me to take the blood samples again.

Thanks to Google Maps, I find the training stables just before lunch. Alan and his team are already waiting.

"Sorry, guys," I say cheerfully to prevent any grumpiness, but I can't overcome the curious stares at me. "We couldn't complete the analysis because we weren't allowed into the building. You know the reason. The police are checking everything."

There is a collective gasp.

"Everything? You mean they are checking the blood tubes, too?" says Alan

"Sure," I say with confidence, to cover the sudden suspicion there might have been something in the blood samples they would rather not be checked.

The same routine as two days ago takes place, a little slower than last time, as I'm taking the blood and labeling the tubes. I don't need my twitch, and one of the stable hands holds the tube rack for me.

"I promise they will be analyzed today. Sorry for the confusion, but I'll send you the results later."

"I'd rather Nerida analyzes the blood and gives us the results, considering what has happened."

"It won't happen again," I say, immediately realizing that this was the wrong thing to say.

"I definitely hope not because otherwise, you won't be able to keep your vets if they get knocked off one every week.'

I laugh, but I know that is also the wrong response to something that was not meant as a joke.

"No offense, but I think you are a little too new at this job yet for us to trust you with our blood results."

"As you wish. I'll let Nerida know as soon as I get back."

With the blood tubes safely in their rack in the back of my SUV, I have time to think about what just happened.

What is going on in this racing stable that they are worried the police might find in the blood tubes or the results? Are they doping their horses for the races? If yes, did Michael know about it? Or do Nerida or Leonard know anything about it? I think I will do a little research tonight about this stable and its racing history.

Back at the hospital, I hand the rack to Nerida.

"They were adamant that it has to be you, and only you, who has to do the analysis of these tubes. They want the results later tonight."

Nerida nods and takes the tubes to the laboratory while Lei rolls his eyes at me.

The rest of the afternoon is busy again. As Leonard warned us, most horses are completely healthy and only need a vaccination or a worm paste to update their annual health maintenance schedule. The clients try to grill me about how Michael died, where he died, and what the police said.

I enjoy disappointing them with the vaguest possible answers until the yard is empty of horse floats.

Chapter 15

Finaly, a bustling day at work, even if the reason for the bustle was Michael's death.

According to the call roster, I am not on tonight. I can enjoy a peaceful dinner and a Google session about the racing stable.

Princess is neighing in her yard for food, and George is impatiently whining to be let out of his run.

"Yes, yes, yes." I rush to complete my pet maintenance chores before sitting down for a cup of tea and a call to Mum.

She wants me to come home, regardless of what happens here. She goes on and on that she never liked Michael, that there were probably more women than men who wanted to see him dead, and that it had probably nothing to do with horses at all.

I just get in the occasional yes and no, but I insist that I stay. I tell her that being thrown in at the deep end and having to do a lot of work now by myself without Michael trying to patronize me is the best thing that could happen to me. Of course, I don't mean that I wished Michael dead. Nothing of the kind.

"Mum, there's something else I want to ask you. What do you know about 'Blue Wren Cottage'?"

There's a long silence at the other end.

"What Blue Wren Cottage?" The question sounds hesitant and vague. But it also sounds like a lie, or at least an attempt to fob me off from asking more questions.

"Yes, the cottage I'm living in is called Blue Wren Cottage, and Nan used to live here with her mother."

"Did she, now?" says Mum slowly. "I don't know anything about that."

"I don't believe you, Mum. You have all been so secretive about your lives that I have no idea about our family history."

"Never mind, Riona, it's nothing special. We're not a special family. We were just an ordinary farming family in the past, and now we've retired to a quiet life in the city. Nothing to be concerned about. I still would prefer it if you came home and found a job in one of the small animal practices here in town."

"It's not going to happen, Mum. I like it here in this little cottage. I'll learn a lot about horse medicine here and find out more about this cottage."

Mum groans. She doesn't like the idea, but I'm not sure whether she just thinks about the murder or about what

I might learn from Nan's notebooks in the green trunk about witchcraft. Or about the history of Blue Wren Cottage.

It's almost dark, and I preheat the oven to bake a frozen pizza.

Rrreow. Rrreouw. Rreoouw.

The sound outside the backdoor tells me that Precious wants to show me a mouse she has caught.

I open the door to praise her but am shocked to find her sitting with her front paw on a rabbit. The rabbit is only a baby rabbit, terrified and frozen in fear under her foot.

"Oh, Precious, why did you have to bring me a rabbit. I don't eat rabbits of the kind you have here. It's far too small to eat and also far too cute. I know rabbits are a pest in this country but I'd prefer if you'd eat them somewhere else, please."

Precious looks at me as if I were daft.

"Come on in, Precious," I say, holding the door open for her. She slowly steps in, completely ignoring the rabbit outside.

"What do I do with you, rabbit?" I ask, scratching my head. The rabbit doesn't give me an answer but darts off into the darkness.

Sipping my cup of tea while waiting for the oven to heat, I settle down in the comfy chair next to the fireplace to think about the day. Precious doesn't wait to be invited and jumps up on the armrest for a bit of cheek scratching.

"What do you think about him?" Nan whispers beside me on the other side of the fireplace.

I jolt up, disturbing Precious, who offendedly jumps on the floor. Is this going to be a regular occurrence? Every time I sit down, Nan's ghost appears to talk to me.

"Nan, you scared me, and you scared the cat."

"Relax!" she says. "You don't need to worry about me. Or her. But what do you think about him?"

"What him? Leonard? I don't particularly like him. He's my boss, and neither he nor I care whether we like each other. Chief Conductor policeman? He's okay, I think."

"No, I mean your neighbor."

"What about him?"

"I think he is a nice young boy."

"Yes, but he's not a boy. And he might be a murderer, too. He's the only one I can see with a grudge against Michael."

"Far from it," says Nan. "He is not the only one. He is definitely not the most important one in the lineup of people with grudges."

"Oh, Nan, I have no idea, and I don't know if I want to know about other people's grudges against Michael."

"You might have no choice but to dig a little deeper into that mystery."

"Why, Nan? I'm here to be a vet, not a detective. I don't know how to be a detective."

"But you need to be prepared to defend yourself, just in case."

"In case of what, Nan? The killer attacking me? I haven't been here for longer than five minutes; I haven't made any enemies."

She doesn't answer, maybe because I sound impatient and slightly annoyed. I get up and put the pizza in the oven. Twelve minutes. I fire up my computer and search for the racing stable's name. Their website tells me that it is owned by a company and is managed by the man I have now met twice. It is a big enterprise with both breeding and racing establishments. They have three hundred mares to breed, sell about a hundred yearlings a year for racing, and another hundred for breeding. Their racing stable trains the rest of the yearlings into race-horses. They have operations in all states of Australia.

I read the history of the stud and the racing estab-lishment. The gallery of their most famous racehorses is impressive and boasts many famous horse names. It turns out that they are one of the three most successful racing enterprises in the country and were most success-ful during the last five years in our state.

Ping, says the oven, and I retrieve the pizza. Nothing special, but better than going to a lot of trouble cooking for one person.

While I eat, I keep scrolling. Maybe there were scandals in the past about drugs or money laundering? But, I don't find anything that could count as evidence of any wrongdoing, though there are plenty of unhappy competitors and innuendos in media articles related to racing and breeding.

Interesting. But how would Michael be involved in something like race-fixing or doping?

I need to learn more about drugs for race-fixing. That means digging out my pharmacology and toxicology books that are still in one of the cardboard boxes in my bedroom.

"You might want to take a look at some of my notebooks too," says Nan next to my ear. I drop the pizza triangle on the keyboard as I jump from the sudden Nan interference. "It might be quicker than going through your textbooks because some of these thugs go with the olden-day rackets instead of newfangled drugs."

"I will, Nan. But tonight, I think I'll try something else. I want to see if I can figure out how to get into Michael's flat in the mansion to see if I can find any clues there. He lived there after he moved out from here. Was he friends with Leonard? Did they work together with the trainers? Maybe I can find something useful. I think I'll go and have a look."

"Oh, no! Don't do that. Wait until you are more familiar with the whole situation."

"What situation, Nan? You're making me even more curious now and making it sound so dangerous. Maybe I'll wander over to the mansion after work tomorrow instead," I say.

"I wouldn't do that if I were you. Leonard doesn't like it if staff goes to the house or even just beyond the boundary of the hospital premises."

"But I'm new, and I don't know where the boundaries are, so he can't blame me."

"You wouldn't be able to get in through the gate without a special pass anyway. It's the big, tall gate in the hedge behind the stallion yard. You can't miss it. That's the boundary. Don't pretend you haven't been warned," says Nan, laughing nervously. It sounds like teaspoons rattling in a cutlery drawer.

"Yes, Mam, I consider myself warned," I say, giggling. "I promise to stay here tonight. Nite Nite, Nan."

Chapter 16

I have no intention of listening to Nan. Precious stares at me while George stares at my pizza slice, hoping to get at least a little bite of it.

"Yes, Precious, let me have dinner first. We need to wait until it's dark, and then I promise I will check out the mansion."

According to the roster, Janice is on tonight, but I don't expect anyone to appear at night for a consult. So she will be in the staff room, either sleeping or watching TV.

Precious impatiently watches me eating my dinner, sitting like a statue and following each bite from the plate to my mouth, her tail slowly oscillating from left to right and back.

She must wonder why it takes me so long to eat, but I need to pass the time until I think it's late enough for Janice to bunk down in the staff room for the night.

After washing the dishes and stacking them in the wooden drying rack, I go through Nan's book on poisonous plants. It can't hurt to know what grows here and what to be careful of.

I am sure Leonard is not asleep yet, either. It will take me at least five minutes to walk around the hospital buildings in the dark. Should I take George with me? I can always say I was looking for him if I get caught out. But he might spook that stallion, so it's better to leave him at home and lock him in his run.

After waiting another hour, I set off in the dark.

"Precious? Where are you? Come on, give me a hint where I need to go. I guess the gate to the mansion must be near the hospital building. Come on, Precious, show me the way."

Out of the dark, Precious appears and weaves around my legs.

"Go on, Precious, let's go."

Precious trots off in front of me.

Luckily, the moon is still three-quarters full, and the winding brick path to the hospital is level, without deceiving potholes. There is no wind at all, and I can hear Rocky's dogs barking faintly in the distance. It is amazing how far sounds carry. That means there were really no sounds the night when Michael died. I would have heard them. So why did my animals spook so much? I walk across the car park, trying to stay out of the motion sensors that make the carpark lights come on when they detect movement.

I am unlucky and suddenly covered in bright light. Quickly, I run to the wall of the clinic building, stumbling over the border of the small garden bed alongside it, and wait for the lights to go off again. It takes a while for my eyes to adjust to the dark after the bright light. I can see blood tubes being automatically tilted back and forth in the analyzer in the lab. That means that either Leonard or Janice is going to come back to read the results sooner or later.

I can't see Precious, but I am now curious enough to explore without her help. I'm sure she'll turn up in case I get lost.

Creeping along the walls, I reach the horse wash and then the stallion yard. The stallion has detected me and stands at the rails, staring in my direction silently, head held high, and ears pricked.

Should I run past him to the gap that I can see in the huge cypress hedge? This gap is the gate to Leonard's yard. As I creep closer, I see the vertical bars of the tall steel gate forbidding my entrance to the mansion's grounds. The bars are too close together to squish through. I need to find another way to get in there and past the stallion. But he doesn't like creeping people and utters a loud warning snort.

It's quite a scary sound—short, brash, and powerful. I stand up and walk past him as if I were just another stable hand like Tilly or Lorna, doing the rounds at night. He follows along on the inside of his yard as I pass by toward the far end of the hedge. It seems to go on forever, extending into the dark distance. Searching for another entrance to the mansion, I finally find a large hole in the hedge.

It's cut into the huge, overgrown hedge like a doorway, and I enter cautiously. The untrimmed hedge is taller than I am with outstretched arms, probably over fifty years old. I walk forward and straightaway run face-first into another hedge. It seems to be a tunnel in the hedge, which I follow to the left, only to be led around a ninety-degree corner to the right.

What is this? After a few more deviations, I conclude that I'm working my way through a maze.

Darn! It's so dark, and the hedge is so tall that I can't see over it. I can't even see the moon now. After a few twists and turns, I am completely lost. Then I remember I read somewhere that to find the way out of a maze, you must put one hand on a wall and keep following that wall around all corners until you are out of the maze.

I use my left hand and follow along the scratchy cypress hedge wall. After a few minutes of careful progress, I stumble into an open square. This seems to be the middle of the maze. Now what? I can see the moon now and can also see that from this square space, there are four routes out. I need to choose one of the three that are right, left, and in front of me to find my way into Leonard's yard, but which one?

I take the left one, keeping my left hand to the wall, and it turns out that it is a dead end. I end up back at the center square. While I try to reach the opposite exit, my foot trips into a hole.

"Ouch! Darn, I've twisted my ankle," I swear aloud and hop up and down on the spot to loosen it up again. I can't afford another trip to the hospital.

I hear Princess neigh in the distance, and then the stallion answers outside the maze. But she does not answer him back. Maybe he told her where I am?

Against my better judgment, I use my phone camera to see what I tripped over. There is a giant rabbit warren in the middle of the maze with several holes, dead ends, and fake entrances. I switch off the camera and carefully move forward to the opposite exit on the other side of the warren, careful not to trip again.

"Meeh!"

"Precious! Is this what you wanted me to find?" I whisper to the cat, who winds herself around my boots back and forth as if to stop me from going any further.

I ignore her antics. I'm here to see what's behind the hedge and follow the path that might lead to an exit opposite Leonard's mansion. After a few minutes, I can see lights. I pop my head outside the hedge, hoping that no watchdog waits to bite my face off.

Chapter 17

Everything outside the hedge looks peaceful. The bright three-quarter moon shows the double-story mansion in its full glory in the middle of manicured lawns and illuminated garden beds. The building is old, but it must have been restored some time ago. The wraparound verandah, both on the ground level and the upper story, reminds me of Como House in South Yarra. Electric lighting along the veranda allows anyone to take a stroll around the house and gardens in the evening without breaking their legs.

A footpath leads from the mansion to a large corrugated iron shed. Though I can't hear any sounds coming from that building, the brightly lit skylights and row of parked white vans indicate that people are working there during the night. How strange.

I stand up, admiring the serene garden landscape around the mansion, wondering where the entrance to Michael's flat might be. One of the floor-to-ceiling doors at ground level is open. A woman plays her cello next to a silent grand piano in a large, parqueted room with a chandelier above her head. She does not have a music stand in front of her so must play from memory. I cannot see her face, but her long gray hair and mature figure give me the impression she is old enough to be Leonard's wife, Olga.

I stand in awe of the melancholy sound of the cello, frozen in time, and the mood of the composer's ideas. I feel Precious beside me as she skips around in the open, the black and orange colors of her fur bright and rich in the moonlight while her white tuxedo markings make her appear like a puppet on strings skipping on a stage.

Suddenly, the floodlights turn on. Leonard has installed enough of them on the second-floor balcony to turn the place to simulate complete daylight.

"Darn and darn again! Shooo, Precious!"

I turn and realize I have moved more than ten meters toward the cello music from my maze exit. I gallop back toward it and dive into the hedge when a couple of dogs approach at full speed, a large German Shepherd and a Jack Russell Terrier.

Oh Shivers! What do I do now? I run around a few of the maze's corners when I hear Precious scream the most terrifying cat battle cries. It sounds like a battalion of cats and dogs fighting in the dark.

Crouching and squeezing myself between two hedge plants, I hope that I won't be detected if the dogs find their way into the maze.

Then I see the lights of a torch flicker toward the maze and into the branches. Leonard is calling off his dogs.

"Blooming cats! Leave them!" he yells, but the dogs are persistent. They don't want to give up. I hear Precious scream again in an atrocious cacophony of feline fury.

Leonard yells at the dogs a few more times, and finally, the three of them disappear toward the house. I start breathing again, my heart in my throat, but don't dare to move yet. It's eerily quiet n, but then I realize that the cello has not stopped at all. The music is still a haunting melody of anguish and sadness.

Leonard's front door slams shut, but the woman keeps playing.

My thoughts turn to how I can find my way out of the maze without attracting the dogs' attention, but then I feel Precious beside me.

"Mee," she says. I reach for her and feel her warm fur. It seems she's not reassured at all but is anxious to get out of here. She moves along the maze path in front of me, around the corners, and stops at the rabbit warren.

"What now? Precious? What is it about this rabbit warren?"

I switch on my phone light again and shield its beam with my left hand. I point it to the ground and into every warren hole that I can see.

"I can't see anything, Precious. There is nothing here."

She does not budge and keeps looking into the biggest entrance into rabbit city. And then I see the brief blink of a reflection of glass. I stretch my hand deeper into the warren but cannot reach what is in there. I take a photo and hope that helps me see.

The photo is not brilliant. It is almost invisible, but I can see the outline of something small and rectangular. Precious walks over and sits next to the hole. Another photo, and I can see the reflection of Precious's white tuxedo markings on the small screen of a mobile phone.

"Precious, do you know what that is? We might have found Michael's phone."

She gives me 'The Look' again as if to say, 'I found it, and you needed a lot of coaxing to follow me to it.'

"Never mind, Precious. What do we do now? Do we leave it here, or do we take it home and call the Chief Conductor?"

I decide to leave the phone where it is. It is not looking like rain and it is unlikely that Leonard's dogs would find it in a hurry. They hadn't found it thus far. But someone either dropped it here on purpose or by accident and might come back to find it.

Time to call Nan and get a hint from her as to what to do, but I decide to do that from home and not here, exposed to being found in a place where I'm not meant to be.

"Come on, Precious, let's go home." She doesn't need to be asked twice and I follow her until we end up in the open again next to the stallion yard.

"Phew! Thank you, Precious. What would I do without you?"

The stallion ignores us as we slink past him and creep along the hospital building to stop the floodlights from coming on again. The blood tubes in the lab have stopped moving, which means that Leonard or Janice must have been here while I was in the maze.

It takes me only about two minutes to get to the cottage and here we are, home again. I kick off my boots, let George into the cottage, and dive onto the chair next to the fireplace, hoping that Nan might appear.

But after a few minutes of silence, I go to bed. Sleep escapes me for a while because my mind can't let go of the woman with the cello.

Chapter 18

Bleary-eyed, I make myself breakfast. My last two pieces of toast. I need to go shopping today. At least there is no shortage of coffee and tea, thanks to the box of goodies that Mum packed for me.

After a total revamp of my appearance in the bathroom, a new set of jeans, and a dark blue shirt, I am ready for work. The cello music is still playing in my head as I feed Princess. She seems a bit standoffish today. Maybe she was worried during the night when I heard her call.

At the hospital, Nerida and Lei man the fort and I'm rostered for outside calls. Most of the bustle at the hospital has subsided again. Amy has scheduled only two clients to come in, and no outside calls yet.

I am unsure what to do, so I watch Nerida and Lei treating the two horses that arrived yesterday during the rush for information about Michael's death.

Janice is tidying up the pharmacy shelves to avoid talking to anyone. I feel not only superfluous but like a complete waste of space today.

What is it with these people? What do they know that makes them behave this way? Nobody talks even though thousands of unanswered questions are hanging in the air.

A car pulls up outside. In anticipation of a potential client, I rush to open the roller door of the breezeway.

"Good morning, Miss Clay," says Chief Inspector Brown. "I am glad I found you here. It saves me the way to your cottage."

"Glad to see you too, Chief Conductor Brown." I giggle to break the ice. Why is he glad to see me? I pretend not to be concerned. "Any news about Michael yet?"

He glares at me, and I realize I called him Conductor instead of Inspector.

"Sorry, Chief Inspector, you remind me so much of my school's orchestra conductor. I will try to not be so rude again."

"Never mind. There is no need for you to apologize for that minor detail. I have larger fish to fry. How about you accompany me to the station for a formal interview?"

"Me? Why me? I don't know anything about anything and nothing about Michael in particular. You interviewed me already, didn't you?"

Nerida, Lei, and Janice have stopped moving and stare at me as if I have grown a set of horns in the last five minutes.

"You will find out soon enough. Now, it's time to get moving. I don't want to put handcuffs on you if I can avoid it. It would be so undignified for someone who calls me Chief Conductor."

I follow him toward his car.

"What about Leonard? I have to tell him I won't be here for call-outs."

"No, there is no need for that. I talked to him already."

The drive to Green Bowlder town passes without a word. My attitude toward Mr. Brown has changed. I doubt his intelligence and judgment, considering he sees me as a suspect in Michael's murder. His frizzy conductor's hairdo now seems just like an oversized mullet tied up in a Bogan man bun. Nothing of a romantic or sophisticated nature.

He opens the glass door to the police station, a seventies-style orange brick veneer building that is part of the Green Bowlder council offices, and then the door to a small, bleak room with a square table and three chairs.

"Have a seat! Coffee?"

"Yes, please, black, no sugar," I say and sit down.

He returns with two coffees and a female police officer, who I assume is supposed to become the witness to my confession.

"Now, let's start at the beginning," he says after the preliminaries of the date and time and participants in the interview.

"What beginning?" I ask.

"When did you meet Michael first?"

"You mean here at the hospital or in my life years ago?"

"Let's start years ago, if that suits you better. That might give me an idea about motive."

"I have no motive, to state the obvious. I met him when we both started in the same year at the University of Sydney six years ago. We lived in the same college."

"What College was that?"

"King's College. He became the house Prefect straight away because he supposedly had shown leadership at school and in sports, and therefore, he threw his weight around from day one."

"So, you resented him."

"As did most other people there."

"How did he throw his weight around?"

"We had an open-door policy where anyone could invite themselves into your room to talk and be friends, but only during the daytime. But he tried it on with most girls at night, too."

"I see. With you too?"

"Of course. I was female, so he felt entitled to come in at any time. But I kicked him out every time. In the end, I reported him because he became too handsy. He stopped coming into my room, but he patronized and bullied me in any other way possible for the whole first year I was there. That's why I took a gap year and went to Europe."

"What about your studies? He seemed to have finished his studies well before you. How is that possible?"

"Some of my family are from Europe, and my parents wanted me to be more proficient in the German language. There is also a long tradition of horse medicine in our family. I spent most of my time in Germany riding horses. I really enjoyed my gap year there."

"I see, but that doesn't explain two years of difference."

"No, after graduation, I had a serious horse-riding accident that left me in a coma for weeks and in rehab for almost an entire year. After that, I found it hard to find a job straightaway because people imagined I was incapacitated and had no stamina. Nobody wanted to give me a job."

"I see. So, why do you think Leonard employed you?"

"I have no idea. I don't understand it at all. There's not enough work for six vets."

"Five vets?"

"Six. Nerida, Molly, Lei, Janice, Michael, and me. I can see hardly anything happening here, so I have no clue at all."

"Could Michael have recommended you to Leonard because he wanted to catch up with you again?"

"No, he was just as surprised to see me on my first day here as I was to see him."

"Did he seem happy to see you?"

"No, not at all."

"Tell me a little about your work interactions and the day you worked together."

I described our drive to and from the training stable and how we took blood samples. I described my surprise that Michael could afford a three hundred thousand dollar Raptor because first and second year out of vet school vets don't get paid much. Even though he lived in the cottage for free before me, the Raptor was a mystery to me.

Chief Inspector Brown nods, pondering my point.

Chapter 19

"**N**ow tell me again what happened after you came back from your call out to the trainers."

"By the time we were back, it was the end of the work day, and we all went home. At least I went home to feed my horse and my dog and unpack my things."

"I see."

"That reminds me—do you think I will be home before dark today? If not, I need to ask someone to feed them for me."

"Why do you think you might not be at home before dark? Do you think you have so much to tell us it takes that long? Interesting!"

"No, there is nothing to tell. But it might be better if I call the neighbor to come over to feed them. Is that ok with you?"

"By all means, go right ahead. But please put your phone on speaker for me."

I tap Rocky's number into my mobile, and he answers right away.

"Hey, Rocky, I'm in town at the police station for an interview, and I'm on speaker, if you don't mind."

"I don't mind; what's up, Riona?"

"They might keep me here for a while until they are satisfied I am not a suspect in Michael's murder. If I'm not home by dark, do you mind going over and feeding the horse and the dog? Feed is in the tack room for the horse and the kitchen for the dog."

"Sure, if I see your lights on, I'll know you're back, and I'll stay home. If not, I'll jump over the fence and feed them. Are you ok?"

"Yes, I am. Nothing to worry about. Thank you, Rocky."

"So, you know Rocky's number off by heart?"

"Correct. He wrote it down on a piece of paper for me and I memorized it straight away. I have a photographic memory since my accident. Everyone knows that."

"I see. Now that we have established that fact, please tell us how Michael happened to show up at your cottage on the day he died."

"On the day he died? He did not die that day. He went home, and he texted me at four the next morning."

"You are mistaken, Miss Clay. When did you say he left your cottage?"

My mind's wheels spin, but I can't make sense of that statement. Do they think Mike died the previous day?

"He left at around 8:30 in the evening and said he was going to process the blood samples we had taken in the afternoon."

"How can you be so sure, Miss Clay? Have you got any witnesses that he left at that time? The mysterious Rocky, perhaps?"

"He definitely left at that time, and he sent me a text at four in the morning."

I pick up my mobile and scroll up the texts of that day.

"Here, you can see. Michael texted me three minutes past four." It was the only text of that day.

Chief Inspector Brown takes the phone and reads the text. He then dictates that he has read the text and reads it out. I lean back in my chair, arms crossed, convinced that this is enough to let me go home.

"There is only one irritating issue with this text. Michael died, according to the pathologist, between 9:00 and midnight. So, he can't have sent you the text."

I stare at him, mouth open.

"How is that possible?" I ask.

"It's possible that someone else sent it. Could that someone have been you? After you killed Michael?"

I have no answer except to say that I'm not strong enough to kill someone as big and strong as Michael.

"Well, are you sure you don't want to amend your statement here?"

"No, I had nothing to do with Michael's death. Nothing at all."

"I beg to disagree, Miss Clay," says the Chief Conductor in a neutral voice, as if he has sufficient evidence that I am the heinous killer of Michael. I swallow nervously.

"You see, Miss Clay, there is evidence you attacked Michael, and we believe you proceeded to kill him after your attack."

"What attack? I didn't attack anyone." What a ridiculous idea.

Mr. Brown opens the folder before him and pulls out a printout of a picture. He pushes it in front of me.

"Can you tell me what that is? I am sure you can explain this little detail here on Michels's thigh."

I am speechless. Michele's thigh bears the imprint of my twitch. It appears he was struck with the twitch, and the number 1870 engraved itself in a mirror image on his skin.

I stare at it, speechless. How did that get there? And then I realize how. I laugh and lean back in my chair. But it seems the Chief Inspector does not like my laugh, at least at this point in time.

"That does not sound like an appropriate response to me, Miss Clay. This is an imprint of your twitch gadget, isn't it?"

"Yes, that is an imprint of my twitch gadget, as you call it, but I did not attack him with it."

"Enlighten me then, Miss Clay. But be warned, there are also traces of blood on his clothing.

I take a deep breath and start explaining.

"When Michael arrived, he was in a foul mood, nit-picking at my animals, the cottage, and the cottage decor. He sat in the living room on the sofa, pontificating about how the neighbor was a dog-shooting savage and that I should keep my nose out of the clinic's business. He didn't explain what that business was. I was preparing dinner, a big steak my mother had packed for my first day of work, as a celebration. I had potatoes and a couple of nice ripe tomatoes sitting on the kitchen table. And two eggs. The griddle pan was nice and hot, ready for the steak, when Michael appeared in the kitchen. He told me I should invite him, but I said he should go home. He called me a cold witch and grabbed me around the waist. This had always been his favorite trick in the past. Grab the girl when her hands are full of something else. I contemplated planting either the griddle pan, a tomato, or the steak on his face to get rid of him. I chose the steak. When I lifted it from the table, George, my dog, thought he would grab it from my hand but ended up throwing both Michael and me off balance. In the stumble, the twitch rolled from the table and onto the floor, and the eggs, too. They broke, and Michael slipped on the mess, landed on the floor, and I on top of him. He must have landed on the handle of the twitch. Any blood on him is probably from the steak."

I could see the female police officer smirk at that description.

"And then what happened?" says Mr. Brown, glaring at his assistant.

"Michael left, swearing all hell and evil down on me. But even though he was mad, he did not slam his Raptor's door. He closed it nicely but then roared out of the driveway, spitting gravel on me while I watched him leave."

"And that is all?"

"That is all."

"Do you mind if we write that all down, and you sign it as an accurate description of what happened on that day? We will also need your phone to investigate if you had other contacts with Michael or other co-conspirators in this murder."

"I don't mind giving you my phone, but I need it back tomorrow for work."

"They must have a spare phone at your hospital until you can have yours back."

"What about Michael's phone?" says the policewoman. "She could use that."

How do I respond to that? I know that his phone is in the rabbit warren, or at least a phone is in there, but how would I explain that I know where it is. I pretend I have no clue about its whereabouts.

"Don't you need his phone to investigate his texts and calls as well?" I suggest. "I don't really want to use Michael's phone because he's dead, and it would be spooky."

"There is only one problem with that, Miss Clay. We couldn't find Michael's phone anywhere. We need to have a detailed search of your cottage and the veterinary hospital."

"But in the meantime, I can go home, can't I? Because his phone is not in my cottage. It was used after he left from there that evening. So, it must be somewhere else." Maybe I can entice them to search in the hedge.

"If you killed Michael, you could have sent this message to yourself with his phone."

"But I didn't kill Michael, and I did not send that message."

"Well, we can't take your word for it. One of our K9s and his handler are already waiting outside to do the search when we drop you off at your cottage. Come along, Miss Clay."

The interview ends; I read the printout of the interview and sign it as a true representation of what I said.

The Chief Inspector politely opens the back door of his car for me. The K9 German Shepherd is in a separate car, and together, our little convoy takes me back home.

Chapter 20

P recious turns into a dog-sized furry orb and disappears round the corner of the house. Obviously, she disapproves of the dog yapping at the end of his leash for the search to begin.

The handler with the K9 enters first to ensure I don't interfere with their search.

"Don't you need to show the dog something that belonged to Michael to let him find the phone?" I wonder aloud.

"No, this is an electronics dog who is trained to find anything electronic.

"How interesting. He will find my laptop, no doubt. It sits right on the kitchen table. Can I watch him through the door, please? I would love to see how he finds it." I push the front door fully open so that the bullet hole becomes invisible from the inside.

"Sure," replies the Chief Inspector as we wait by the front door. From there, I can see the kitchen table with the laptop. The dog sniffs around the kitchen and then sits, looking up at the tabletop.

"He found it, yay!" I say, with as much sarcasm as I can muster.

The handler praises the dog generously, and he resumes his search in the living room. He sniffs amongst the sofa cushions and in the corners but shows no interest in the hidden door. Another round makes him stop at the green trunk, and he sits, pointing his face at it.

"What the ... " I say.

"Well, well, well. He found more electronics."

"No way," I say.

The dog handler opens the trunk with gloved hands and carefully empties out the contents of the trunk. There are only photo albums and an address book. I'm so glad I moved the book of spells and Nan's notebooks into the hidden room. Mr. Brown would doubt my sanity if he saw any hints of witchcraft.

But then the handler pulls out Nan's spectacle case and holds it up as the dog sniffs at it. He sits down again.

"That's my Nan's spectacles. They don't have electronics in them."

"Let's see." The Chief Inspector walks inside, pointing me to stay in place. They open the case, but I can't see what they've found.

Then the Chief Inspector turns, holding up a mobile phone. Nan's phone, as I can see from the cover, decorated with colorful butterflies.

"That's my Nan's phone," I say. "She left it to me in case I need one." I don't want to sound surprised, even though I'm sure this phone wasn't in the trunk yesterday.

The handler swipes the phone, but it's dead.

I barge in and get the charger from my bedside table.

"Here, put it on the charger. I know her passcode."

They put the iPhone on the charger and push me outside again. The search of my bedroom, the spare bedroom, the bathroom, the car, and the outside of the cottage doesn't reveal the whereabouts of Michael's phone.

"How about the stables?" I suggest.

I lead the way to the stable, where the K9 examines the tack room, tack box, saddle, feed bin, and horse food bag, showing no interest. He looks questioningly at his handler, asking for the next job.

"Let's check the phone to see if it really is your Nan's."

The phone has enough charge to switch it on. They check its details and confirm it isn't Michael's. Thankfully, they're not interested in Nan's pictures and only check when her last text was sent. That was over a year ago, before she died.

"Miss Clay, the dog hasn't found anything of interest here, so we will leave you alone, for now, and continue our search in the hospital buildings."

"That will take a long time because there are a lot of electronics there."

"Do not concern yourself with any of that. We have your mobile, and fortunately, you now have your Nan's so that you won't lose contact completely with the outside world.

I think it's probably more useful for contacting the paranormal world instead of my friends.

There are only two questions burning in my mind. How do I direct the Chief Conductor toward the rabbit warren to find Michael's phone without making him more suspicious of me I decide to consult with Nan first and instead ask the second question.

"How exactly did Michael die? Amy said he was hooked up to the anesthetics machine."

"I can't reveal that to you yet, but I can say his death was not caused by the anesthetics machine."

"I thought it would have been quite impossible to get Michael on the operating table and intubate him like a horse. It would have taken a very strong person to do that because he would have been fighting like hell."

"What an interesting thought. However, that is all conjecture."

I force a friendly smile on my face and wave him and the K9 team goodbye, leaving them to continue their work at the hospital.

Chapter 21

In my mind, I now relegate the Chief Conductor to the class of unfriendly males. I hope I never have to see him again or suffer his less-than-original attempts at humor.

But on one point, he was right. A few minutes later, Rocky's Nissan meekly beeps at the fence. I amble over, not too fast, to ensure he doesn't get the impression I'm desperate or enthusiastic about seeing him.

It's almost dark now, and the day has turned into a purple-grayness.

"Everything alright? They obviously let you go. So, you must be innocent."

I laugh, trying to sound relaxed.

"Did you ever doubt that? How could you! Yes, they let me go, but they kept my phone to check whether I had any contact with Michael. And now I'm cut off from the world without my phone."

"Maybe you'll get it back tomorrow, or you could buy another one in town if they need it for longer."

"Their electronics search dog found my Nan's old phone in a box of goodies she left me. She died a year ago, though, so it's totally out of juice, and it isn't connected anymore."

"At least you only need a new SIM card, then."

"What a great suggestion! I'll do that tomorrow. Thanks for coming over to check on me and my animals."

"Not a problem. Are you good now by yourself?" He turns back to his Nissan.

"Definitely, Rocky, and give my regards to your wife." After the words left my mouth, I could kick myself. This was the world's dumbest and most feeble way of trying to find out whether he has any female attachment at home.

"Wife?" He gives a little laugh before shutting the driver's door and driving off.

Oops! My face turns red. I've put my foot in it again. I just can't imagine him not being taken already.

I feed Princess and George, turning over in my mind Rocky's gray eyes with the slight crow's feet from the sun. No, stop thinking about him, I tell myself. Now, it's time to start thinking about dinner. My supplies are getting thin. Tomorrow is the day for shopping and I'll get a new SIM card for Nan's phone. I see that it's now fully charged with the picture of her orange cat on the screen.

I tap in her passcode, which is my birthdate. Wow! It allowed me access. Nan's phone has so many pictures in its picture folder, and I get lost in her memories, dinner all but forgotten.

I loved my Nan. She was so spunky. Thinking about her brings tears to my eyes, even now. Her texts ended a year ago, and any incoming phone calls since then have gone unanswered, too. I'll keep her orange cat screensaver in memory of her once I get a new SIM.

A sudden vibration and the sound of a horse neighing in my hand give me such a fright that I throw the phone in the air, away from me.

"What the ... ?"

I catch it again before it lands on the floor. It keeps neighing. Nan's ringtone is a neighing horse. It must be live and paid up. Otherwise, it wouldn't ring right now.

It keeps neighing until I answer it.

"Yes?" I say, not wanting to disclose my identity to whoever is at the other end of the call.

"Riona? Is that you?"

I almost fall off my nice, comfortable chair next to the fireplace. It's Nan's voice. A cold chill runs up my back, and my hands shake.

"Yes, it's me. But this can't be Nan. Who is calling?"

"Don't be so suspicious, Darling. I am glad you found the phone and switched it on. We talked before. Yesterday, if you can remember that far back with your mushed-up brain. I have paid for the contract for the next couple of years. I just wanted to make sure you can connect with me until you can stand on two feet in this strange world."

My hands keep shaking. In fact, my whole body shakes now in fear and confusion. I'm glad Rocky has left and doesn't see me in this state.

"What does this mean, Nan? Is this really you? You're truly a ghost, aren't you? Yesterday, you talked to me from this chair, and now on the phone. This is crazy. Why call me on the phone when you can be in this room. Does this mean you can call me anytime on this phone, wherever I am? I am so confused."

"Exactly, that's what it means. And you can call me anytime you need me. There's nothing much that I cannot postpone on this side of the curtain."

My mouth is dry. I can't believe I'm having a conversation with a ghost on a mobile phone. Have I died? Or did my brain suffer a mortal hit when I had my accident? Or has the stress of my police interview affected me? I'm sure this phone wasn't in the green trunk yesterday. How did it get there today?

"You know, the book of spells will come in handy for moving things around once you know how to design spells."

This can't be true. This is not real. I don't believe in ghosts and all this paranormal stuff. I am a science girl. Give me the facts, and I know my way around the most intractable problems. Yesterday's adventure in the maze and hearing the cello music was spooky enough, but still sort of real. But this? What am I supposed to do with this sort of information?

"Wow! But Nan, what can you do from the other side, in case I call you for urgent help? You can't just hop back into life and appear on my doorstep or wherever I call from."

"There is nothing I can do in terms of actions, but you can ask me for advice or information. I have access to many resources here and so many of them can reach over to your side. With more information, you can always make better decisions."

This is all extremely disturbing and not exactly reassuring. I stand up, thinking that moving around my living room will make me feel calmer, but it doesn't work.

"Can I put you on video call, Nan?"

"You can, but I'm not sure you will see much of me."

Switching to video mode there's only a vague outline of my Nan's face, all flickery and noisy. She still looks ninety-eight years old. How disappointing. I thought ghosts would appear young again when they enter reality to avoid scaring their 'victims'. I can see her mouth moving, but her voice has disappeared, so I switch back to voice-only mode.

"Don't worry, Riona. You will get used to it. Now tell me about your day. So much to catch up on. What have you been up to? I've had some negative waves weave into my realm and am a little worried."

I sit down again in the chair next to the fireplace. Sound reception seems to be best in this spot. I sigh, making my legs fold more comfortably under me while telling Nan everything about what has happened since I talked to her last, which was only yesterday. I am glad I haven't started dinner yet because it would be burned by now.

"So, in essence, you think Michael was murdered because he knows something that is dangerous and has to do with the vet hospital? Leonard has a strange wife hidden in the mansion. You can't figure out how Michael died and why the police think you are the main suspect. And there is another building next to the mansion that looks busy at night. But you don't know what they are doing in there."

"That's about it."

"Maybe there are clues in the hospital's computer system. Can you find out more about the clients and how they might be involved in any shady shenanigans with Michael?"

"I can do that tomorrow. I think I'm on call tomorrow."

"Now let me think about this all a little more. I am so glad we found a way to talk now, even when you are not in this room. It makes me much calmer. Good night, Riona."

"Nite Nite, Nan, talk soon."

I don't really feel like eating now, but I think sticking to some sort of routine after the unannounced disturbance of my tranquility by Nan seems to be the best thing to do.

After dinner, an egg and bacon quiche from the freezer, I open the hidden room behind the wall panel and scan the spines of Nan's notebooks. Intrigued by the 'Book of Spells', I take it off the shelf.

It can't hurt to find out a little more about this witches' business if I'm supposed to converse with Nan. I should know more about what she was up to, and maybe I'll learn something useful, too. It may all be some ridiculous mumbo-jumbo, but I am still curious. Maybe I can learn to move things around with spells. That would be kind of fun to do.

The book is thin, twenty pages at most. I'm glad because I don't think at this time of the night, and in my mental state, complicated spells are what I can process.

The first page informs me that the book belonged to Friederike Woynewitch, nee Radtke. Under her name, I read the name Elena Anderson, nee Woynewitch, Nan's mother. Under Elena's name is the name Anastasia Anderson, my Nan. Does this mean I now have to write my name under hers? What about my mother's name? I need to ask Nan why Mum's name is not in this book.

From the way Mum reacted to my question about the cottage, I could guess she didn't want to know anything about her witch family. Or she doesn't want to share whatever she knows. Poor Mum, she only wants to be like everyone else; her idea of normal.

But do I want to be a witch? Is that something that I could or should aspire to? I always knew I wanted to be a vet. I was one hundred percent sure about that. I never thought I wanted to be anything else. Now, I'm supposed to be a witch? Can one be both, if I find it attractive to become a witch? I shiver as if her ghostly fingers had stroked my shoulder. It felt like the lightness of butterfly wings.

I leaf through the book of spells, trying to decipher the writings of the three women in their particular styles. Friederike's old-style German spells are written in now yellowing, faded ink, Elena's in strong strokes, and Nan's in expansive style, covering the notebook's lines and pages. There are plenty of empty pages at the end of the notebook for future generations of witches. Unless all

possible spells have already been cast and documented.
I need to ask Nan about that, too.

Chapter 22

I wake up apprehensive and tense, and drag myself out of bed. This must have all been a dream.

While grinding and brewing my coffee, I stare at Nan's phone as if it's a poisonous toad, doubting my own mind. There is a way to check whether Nan and I used the phone. I check the call register, and with a sigh of relief, I put it back on the kitchen table. There are no calls listed, and my image in the bathroom mirror shows me that I am not sick. It must have all been a dream.

But why is my mind tricking me into hearing Nan and even seeing her on the phone screen? I'm not ready to accept that either I'm nuts or that I can see and talk with ghosts. Somehow, deep down, I know I'm not nuts, so I need to come to grips with the fact that I can converse with Nan, at least in my mind. But why did she have to turn up right now? As if life wasn't difficult enough already.

Tending to Princess gives me a sense of sanity that's been missing since Nan's phone call. The grass in her yard is getting scarce. I need to buy some hay for her;

maybe Rocky will sell me some. While I collect Princess' manure, move the wheelbarrow along, minding my own business, relaxed, and enjoying the clear and almost windless weather, the phone vibrates and neighs in my back pocket. Princess answers with an enthusiastic greeting from the other end of the yard and gallops over to me. Her nose nuzzles my back pocket as I pull it out from under her determined nose. I am shaking in my Blundstones now.

"What is this?" I press the green button to answer it.

"Is that my horse answering my phone call?" Nan laughs loudly, and Princess appreciatively nickers an answer. She almost pushes me over just to stay in nose contact with the phone.

"Nan, you gave me the fright of my life. Again. How can you call from the other side, and me and the horse can hear you? This is insane. I don't want to talk to a ghost when I'm around people. They might think I'm crazy."

"I won't call you when you are around people, and you don't need to answer if you don't want to. I am not that inconsiderate. But I think you need a bit of company out here. You don't appreciate your companions yet that look after you without you knowing."

"Which companions?"

"Precious and Princess, as you call them. Precious is your proper familiar. You need to pay attention to what she says to you. It might save your life one day."

"Familiar? Don't be so melodramatic, Nan." She keeps talking as if I had not interrupted her.

"Precious is your helper from the paranormal side of the equation. She was my mother's and my familiar while we lived in the cottage. She didn't want to leave when we had to move. That's why I got Boris once we were in town. He was our familiar in Russia. "

"You really lived here? In this cottage? Why? Princess, stop milling around me. You can't eat this phone."

"About the horse," continues Nan. "Princess was my horse, and I sent her to you after your accident, so you had a horse to love while you recovered. She is not quite the experienced familiar yet, but with time, she might get there. She's a horse, after all, and they need a little more patience than cats, or owls, for that matter."

I put the wheelbarrow away and give Princess her small scoop of pellets. Finally, she decides breakfast is better than a chat with ghostly Nan.

"Nan, I love Princess, Precious, and George, but I need to go to work with a clear mind without distractions from familiars and ghost appearances on my phone. We might talk tonight."

"Roger, over and out!" Nan laughs, and the phone goes quiet.

I lock George up in his dog run, hoping he is not one of Nan's previous familiars, too, who would take being locked up as an affront. My black coffee lasts for the few minutes till I arrive at the hospital building, where I am the last to arrive, even though I live the closest.

My mood darkens when I see the Chief Conductor's easily recognizable car. Why is he here now? I try to avoid him by entering through the breezeway of the stable, but I have no luck. There he is, standing in front of the drug cupboard, having an intense discussion with Leonard.

I try to sneak past, but the Chief Conductor seems to have eyes in the back of his head.

"Hi, Miss Clay; I wonder if you could explain to me some of these drugs that Dr. Scott has so kindly lined up for me on the bench here.

Drats. With pretend confidence, I greet him, noticing he wears white trainers with his dark suit. What fashion magazine influenced that choice?

"Hi, Chief Conductor; what brings you here so early in the morning?"

He looks at me as if I were a dangerous spider or a devious criminal trying to trick him into believing in my skills of deception. Is he suspicious of me because I call him Chief Conductor instead of Chief Inspector?

"You still want to pretend you don't know how your friend Michael died?"

"He wasn't my friend, and I don't know how he died."

At last, he will tell me. Curiosity might kill a cat, but not me. I wait patiently for him to enlighten me.

"He had enough drugs in his system to kill a horse."

"What drugs?"

"You tell me. You probably know what to use to kill a horse."

"We use what people commonly call the 'Green Dream', but that's nothing one would want to use for committing suicide."

"I didn't say it was suicide. Michael was injected with a cocktail of drugs, and it wasn't your so-called 'Green Dream.'"

Leonard looks at me with a fake blank expression as if this crazy conversation doesn't concern him. Maybe he thinks I'm an idiot, and I don't know the drugs used in horse medicine.

"Perhaps, Miss Clay, you could tell me what drugs you would use if you wanted to knock out someone as strong as Michael."

"Now, Chief Inspector, you can't do that. You are trying to make her speculate about something that she has no experience in. I explained to you we do not use this cocktail of drugs for horses in this country. Least of all in the proportions you said were used to kill Michael."

"We'll check your pharmacy, cupboards, and vets' cars against your logbook and billing."

"Sure, let's get started so we can finish as soon as possible. Why don't you start with Riona's car so that I can send her out on calls as soon as you finish? I can have the other vets wait until you have searched their cars before we tackle the treatment cupboard here and the pharmacy room."

I open the door to the hold-all in the back, unlock the drug box, and pull out all the drug packages. The police officer makes a list of the drugs and states that they were never opened.

No wonder since I had no calls where I would have needed to use any anesthetics or tranquilizers at all.

Both Leonard and the Chief Inspector are satisfied and let me be.

"Riona, you need to drive out to Alan again and drop off some treatments for a couple of horses. You took blood samples from them yesterday. I have prepared and boxed them up for you in reception."

"See you later, Chief Inspector," I say cheerfully. "Or better not."

He doesn't acknowledge me, and I turn to collect the box from Amy, who keeps her eyes glued to her computer screen, typing up invoices.

"Did they tell you how Michael died? It's so unreal," I say, hoping that Amy can shed some more light on how and when it happened. But Amy shrugs her shoulders and has nothing to add.

On the way to the training stable, I use the time to speculate how Michael might have received a lethal injection of a horse tranquilizer cocktail.

I can't imagine he would have volunteered for an intravenous drip or injection, so it must have been an injection in the muscle. I can only imagine someone surprised him with a jab before he could take evasive action.

He would have gone down quickly with no time to find an antidote, even if he'd known what to use. Probably, the killer would have just stood by and watched, then hoisted him on the operating table using the horse crane.

This means that the murderer knew how to operate that equipment, what drugs to use, and in what quantities. It can only be a vet or a vet nurse, and it would have happened in or near the operating theater. Did the murderer have help?

I need to look deeper into motives and connections between the training stable staff and Michael's relationship with our own staff.

As I start my car, Lei suddenly opens the passenger door and jumps in with me.

"Can I come with you to the trainers, please? I have never been there."

"By all means, if it is okay with the Chief Inspector and Leonard."

"They are fine with it."

Chapter 23

On the way to the training stable, Lei tells me that he loves racehorses and wants to learn everything possible about them. Nerida and Michael had always stopped him from meeting Alan. He is excitedly fidgeting in his seat, a curious change in his demeanor as he chats non-stop until we drive through the familiar sandstone gates.

I wonder aloud whether we should just put the box of goodies into their letterbox as Nerida did or whether we should deliver it into the hands of Alan.

Alan could possibly give me a few clues about any problems that they had with Michael or the hospital.

"Why don't you go to reception?" says Lei. "But please don't tell them I work with you. I am just a friend from Hong Kong visiting you."

I love the idea and realize that Lei isn't wearing the hospital uniform with the logo. He looks like a junior businessman on holiday.

"Sure, Lei, this will be fun. Maybe they'll let us watch the training, and you'll be able to see the horses running."

I park the car in front of reception instead of driving to the stables. This may give us other clues about the outfit. The reception area has been designed to impress racehorse owners and buyers. It's large, with a desk island in the far corner. An arrangement of native flowers breathes class and money.

The receptionist, dressed in a dark, tailored suit, ignores me completely and jumps up to greet Lei. I wait for her to invite me to approach the polished desk island. She looks more like a model or an Emirates Airline first-class hostess than someone interested and working with horses.

Her false eyelashes are overly long and adorned with fake diamonds that sparkle every time she blinks. I am fascinated by how she might be able to drink out of a cup with her filler-stretched lips.

Lei pretends to not understand a word she says to me and looks at me as if he were waiting to interpret for me.

"Hi, my name is Riona. I am here to drop off some treatments for a couple of the racehorses. This is Mr. Lei from Hong Kong, a friend of mine. He would like to see the horses, please."

The receptionist looks me up and down, expressionless. She obviously concluded that I'm a stable hand, not to be remembered by name. Her face is flat and unwrinkled, covered in flawless makeup; her botoxed forehead and her overfull lips show me she is putting extra effort into appearing expensive and unique.

"You can leave it here. I'll call Alan, and he'll send someone to pick it up." She points at the furthest desk corner away from her so as not to be contaminated by any horse smell or speck of dirt.

"No, I'd rather not leave drugs just sitting around. I prefer to give them to Alan personally. That's how he would want it, anyway. He might be able to show Mr. Lei some of the horses at the same time."

"Suit yourself, follow the driveway around to the stables. I will call him to say that you are on your way so he can find you in case you get lost. Alan also has brochures on the sales horses if Mr. Lei wants to invest in one of our bloodlines here. "

I give her a vacuous smile and pretend to have forgotten where the door is.

"Not that way!" she says, jumping up from her upholstered chair again and charging as fast as she can on her stilettos to the door behind her to prevent me from entering the building's inner sanctum. She grabs me by the arm and leads me to the door I came in through and opens it for me. I make a point of bumping into her with the twitch on my thigh. She does not flinch, and her filler-enhanced buttocks and thighs feel strange next to me and cause me to stare.

"Errgh," she says, rubbing her hand on her tight black outfit as she closes the door behind me.

At the stable block, Alan looks at me, surprised to see me in the company of an Asian man.

"I didn't expect you here. Rose said some delivery van had arrived."

"Do I look like a van?" I say and give him a friendly laugh. "This is Mr. Lei from Hong Kong. He is a friend of my family and is interested in racehorses."

Lei introduces himself as the nephew of a wealthy Hong Kong businessman who owns horses in Hong Kong. He would love to see how Alan's business and his horses are performing and maybe see a horse or two in action. I watch in amazement as Alan switches from stable manager to a salesman for horses and invites Lei to drive with him around the facilities.

"Hey, Alan," I say. "These are the drugs from Leonard. I didn't know what they were, so I thought it was better to not leave them lying around and falling into the wrong hands,"

A brief expression of suspicion crosses his face. Does he worry about something in the box or something else he'd rather keep a secret?

"There are no dangerous drugs in there. Just a feed additive to balance out their blood electrolytes after the next race. Leonard makes it specifically for each horse, depending on what it needs."

"I'd still rather give it to you, considering what happened to Michael."

"What happened to Michael? He got killed, I know. Any news that you can share?" Alan says, annoyed that I might spoil an opportunity to sell a racehorse to a rich overseas buyer.

"He got injected with a horse drug and died from it. Didn't you know that? I thought by now everyone did and had their theory about it."

"It's the first time I heard about it. But, in hindsight, it's not surprising." Alan appears to be in conflict about how to deal with the situation in the presence of Lei.

My heart skips a beat, and I try to collect my thoughts. Still holding the box with the electrolytes in my hand, I fidget as if my mind is confused.

"Why is that not surprising? He always talked about his adventures and successes. I can't imagine him having any enemies who would have killed him without anyone else knowing who that enemy was. He was such a bragger. He couldn't shut up about his Raptor and how much it cost him to buy it."

"Maybe someone got to him before he could talk about something he shouldn't have talked about. To stop him from talking, I mean."

"I think his secret died with him because the Chief Inspector thinks I killed him."

Alan bursts out laughing.

"That is the best joke I heard all day. Why does he think that?"

"Because I told him I didn't like him. I knew him from his womanizing days at the university."

Lei pretends he does not understand a word of the conversation and stares blankly into the distance, eyebrows raised, as if the conversation about killing someone named Michael would need to be considered if he was going to buy a horse.

"I am quite sure someone else killed him. You don't look strong enough to pull it off. It is a little inconvenient for us that it happened because Michael and Nerida have been our main vets here, and now there is only Nerida. Maybe you need to upskill quickly to step into Michael's shoes."

"I'd rather not fill his shoes. Then I won't meet the same fate as him. I'd rather stay alive for the time being and stay out of his shoes."

"Well, you probably have to avoid making the same enemies that he rubbed up the wrong way. Just keep your nose to the wheel and don't stick it into places you shouldn't, and you probably won't have any problems."

"That is what Michael said to me, too, on my first day at work."

"Did he now?" That question was drawn out into a long pause, which I filled by handing the box of electrolytes to him.

"Never mind for now. Are you going to take Mr. Lei on your guided tour now or do we have to come back some other time? I can wait here until you are back."

"We can do it now," says Alan and leads Lei out to an SUV.

"Make sure you're back soon because I need to help the Chief Inspector sort out our drug cupboards. If you have any new clues about Michael and how I can avoid being tranquilized, call me. I'll give you my phone number."

I write Nan's phone number on the box with the medicines and walk off.

"I'll wait for you in the car," I say to Lei.

Chapter 24

B ack at the hospital, everyone is in a state of shock. The police are still here, with even more police cars than in the morning.

The atmosphere in the hospital had been subdued earlier, with everyone showing pretend optimism about Michael's murder. It must have been an accident or something that someone else did; everyone agreed. There'd be no way one of us in the hospital would be capable of committing such a heinous crime.

But now the atmosphere was different.

"What happened?" I ask Molly, who is a sniveling wreck. Her usually tidy bob has been raked through by her hands into a tangled mess.

"There are drugs missing from the pharmacy. It doesn't tally up with the logbook in reception."

"So? Why are you in such a state? Anybody could have taken them from there."

"But I'm the last in the logbook who checked out tranquilizers."

"So? Do you think the person who took them would have marked them out in the logbook? Don't be ridiculous."

"But they also found out that Michael and I had a relationship and that he broke up with me."

"So? He had a relationship with Nerida, too. He broke up with all the women he had relationships with at Vet School. At least, as far as I know."

"But they think I had motive and opportunity."

"Like every other girl here, I guess. Me excluded, of course, because I didn't know he worked here before I started, and I don't have a key to the heavy-duty drug cupboard in the pharmacy yet."

"Lucky you."

"I wouldn't worry, Molly. The Chief Inspector doesn't really know what he's doing. He takes everyone in one by one to see who confesses. If he takes you in for an interview, he'll let you go tomorrow, trust me."

Trying to distract her, I shift the conversation to a different topic. Maybe she can give me a new explanation for the lack of 'bustling' here.

"Why are there hardly any horses here, Molly? There's really nothing for me to do here. Going out and delivering stuff to the trainers isn't what I thought I was going to do in my career."

"I don't know. It's just quiet sometimes. But if I were you, I wouldn't discuss the trainers and their racehorses with Nerida if I were you. They are clients only of hers, Michael's, and Leonard's. They would never let a newbie loose on the racehorses. Now, it's only Nerida and Leonard. I think Nerida made it clear that you won't be one of the ones to work with them."

"But Leonard sent me out to them today. Why would he do that if he didn't want me to deal with them?"

"I don't know, but Michael always told me to stay out of that trainer's business. He never said why. I found it better to never ask again after he got furious with me when I asked him what the stuff was that he drove out there every week."

"Did you say that to the police?"

"No. That's Leonard's business, not mine."

"I think I'll make myself useful and clean up the laboratory. There's fingerprint powder all over the place. Nothing else to do, and I'm on call after all."

My intention is to see if the blood tubes from yesterday are still in the rack or on the table after being analyzed or whether they have already been discarded in the medical waste.

I plan to spend my time at Amy's computer tonight researching the training stables and their racehorses and seeing where they're going to race on the weekend. With any luck, I can find out whether the stable has the same jockeys riding them regularly, and check who wins.

I am not in luck. The tubes have been disposed of, but then I remember the sheet of paper with the horse's names on it and sort through the paper recycle box, which has escaped emptying.

I rummage through it and retrieve eight blood sampling sheets. I quickly shove them under my T-shirt and take them out to my SUV, where I hide them under the passenger seat foot mat. There are too many horse names to remember just by looking at them in my stressed-out mind. I'll take them home when I go for my dinner before my on-call shift starts.

The police have left, this time with Molly in the Chief Inspector's car. I hope she'll be back later today or at least tomorrow morning. Her frazzled mind would never have been capable of planning and executing the murder of such a formidable person as Michael—unless she had someone helping her. But who could that be? Janice? Lei? Nerida? Leonard? I can't imagine it would be Lei. He's here only for a few months and didn't have enough time to create relationship dramas with Michael and his girlfriends.

Leonard is distracted and just nods when I tell him I'll bunk down on the staff room sofa for my night shift because the police have taken my mobile phone. He disappears toward the big gate in the hedge next to his stallion.

Ambling to Amy's reception desk, as I have nothing better to do, I pretend to be calm and lean my elbows on the counter.

"Amy, I'm on call tonight. Can I use your computer to do some brushing up on the internet on some surgery tricks? I need your password to get in, if that's ok with you. Or you can make a password for me, please."

She nods and writes a password on a piece of paper.

"It's not really my password. It's the reception password. Everyone can use it."

That's great. Everyone can use it. I wonder if there's a log of who signed in on the night Michael died. But then I realize I would only be able to see if there was a login, but not by whom.

Drats. But maybe I can find out what they were looking at on the web.

"Thanks, Amy. I'm going to do some shopping as nothing is happening here. I've run out of fresh food and cat food. I'll be back before everyone leaves."

Hopefully, I'll meet a few new people at the supermarket who are happy to share some local gossip.

Chapter 25

O n the way to my car I pass the horse wash where
Lorna, one of the stable hands, is busy hosing
down her horse after riding.

I hate pretense but decide to chat with her. She might
be interested in sharing some stablehand gossip about
the murder case.

"Do you need any help, Lorna?" I ask. "Are you com-
peting your horse?"

"Yes, I'm trying to get ready for my first competitions in
dressage this year. I've finished Pony Club, and hopefully, my horse will be good enough for Adult Riding Club."

"That's great, Lorna. If you did well in Pony Club, you'll
ace it in Adult Riding."

She beams at me and towels her horse's neck.

"Are you the only one with a horse here, Lorna? Apart
from me, though, because I brought mine with me too."

"I am the only one. Nerida had hers here while
Michael lived in the cottage. She kept it there and took
it to competitions, too. But after Michael moved to

the main house, she sold her horse because she had nowhere close by to keep it."

"Why couldn't she keep it at the mansion when he moved there?"

"I think, by then, they had split up already, and she didn't want to cross paths with him just because of the horse."

"I see. Why did they split up?"

"The usual, I think."

"What is the usual? I thought Michael was a friendly guy. Did he bully her?"

"I don't think so. I mean, 'the usual' is that he never dated anyone for longer than a few weeks or months, then he'd get bored with them and date someone new."

"That sounds familiar. He did the same at university, I heard. Who was the lucky - or unlucky - woman who he ditched Nerida for?"

"None of us here, I don't think. He tried it with all of us, but Leonard put a stop to it and told him he would sack him if he got the stable staff pregnant."

"Lucky you, Lorna. He saved you from the life of a single mum."

Lorna laughs, but I have the feeling she wouldn't have minded being Michael's date. That reminds me that I am, in fact, on the way to the supermarket. Maybe they know more gossip about Michael and his dates.

"I just wonder, if someone from the outside wanted to come and visit Michael in the mansion at night or after hours, how would they have come in? Would Leonard have minded if he had girlfriends over? There is only the gate from the road to the hospital, and then the gate from the hospital to the mansion."

"They could have come from the highway to the mansion, past the manufacturing shed, but it is a long way to walk from there. I think the dogs would have barked."

"It is a mystery," I say and follow her to her horse's yard. "It must have been someone Michael's dog knew, then. Who could it be?"

"Not sure. I don't know. Maybe they got in through the neighbors. But then their dogs would have woken them up if the killer came in through their paddocks." Lorna's idea was possible but not likely.

"How about Rocky, the neighbor with the sheep and cows? Could he be the killer?" I ask in a suggestive tone as if that was the most logical thing to ask. "He had an argument with Michael because of his dog."

"Yes, but Rocky wouldn't hurt a fly. And why would he do it? Michael sold his dog to Leonard as a watchdog, so Rocky didn't have a problem with Michael after that."

"But that doesn't mean that Rocky still couldn't have hated Michael. Maybe about a girlfriend of his?"

A good opportunity to find out if Rocky had any girl-friends.

"Nah, he doesn't hate anyone. He's only interested in his fire brigade trucks and his farm. Most girls wouldn't want to wait forever until he comes around to noticing them."

"So, he couldn't have killed Michael because of jealousy or because he took his girlfriend."

"No, he doesn't have any girlfriend."

"Did Nerida have any new partner after Michael?"

"Nah, she said she would never have another man. They are all bad and can't be trusted."

"She has a point, Nerida, hasn't she. At least as far as Michael goes. But maybe it was a client instead. Maybe someone who wasn't happy with how Michael treated their horse?"

"No, they were all happy with him, as far as I know."

"But we don't have many clients apart from the race-horse trainers and breeders."

"Them? I can't imagine why they would want to kill him."

"You're probably right," I say to Lorna. "Time to knock off and go home, Lorna. I'm going shopping now. Do you need anything from the supermarket?"

"No, thanks for the offer. I'm good."

In the back of my mind appears the image of Botox Rose at the reception desk of the training facility. I can't imagine that Michael would have bypassed such a delicious morsel of female anatomy.

Chapter 26

The supermarket is tiny, with tall, narrow aisles and a limited selection of vegetables that tells me that most who live around Green Bowlder rely on their own veggie patch, not on this sorry lot of plant material. There is the usual variety of frozen food, and that suits me fine. I fill my trolley with frozen pizzas and quiches, pies of the sweet and savory kind, and a box of fish fingers.

The cat food selection is limited so I go by price and buy the most expensive bag of kibble. Precious is, after all, my familiar and deserves the best.

At the checkout sits a woman slightly past middle age. Her hairstyle reminds me of a sixties television house-wife with hair-sprayed blond locks that don't match her gray eyebrows. She gets on her feet as I approach the counter.

"New here?" she asks as she tallies up my goodies.

"Yes, I'm the new vet at the Green Bowlder Vet Hospi-tal."

"Oh, that was quick," she says.

I give her a curious look. "What was quick?"

"Just three days after the vet was killed, you're already here as his replacement."

"No, I was here before he got killed. How do you know he was killed and didn't die just on his own?"

"Grapevine. Nothing stays a secret for long here."

"I see. Maybe you can give me a clue as to why you think he was killed.

"I don't know, but there have been rumors."

"Rumors? About him or about what happened to him?"

"About him more than about what happened."

"Tell me more," I say, taking my time stacking my shopping into an empty cardboard cauliflower box. "It's better being prepared if you're new in a job, if you know what I mean."

She nods and huffs and puffs a little, shifting from one foot to the other behind the cash register.

"He was okay at first when he moved here, but after a while, he got more arrogant. He pretended he was earning a lot of money. But I know the hospital doesn't have many horses or dogs coming in, so I asked him once how he was making his money. He got all cagey and said there are more ways for vets to make money than by stitching up horses and pets. I asked him how, and he said it was nobody's business and certainly not mine."

"Interesting," I say. "I was also wondering why there are so few horses coming in. Why do you think that is?"

"They go to your competition up the road. All the farmers, the Pony Club, and other horse people go there. Your hospital only has racehorses. We don't go there. I took my grandkids' ponies there a couple of years ago because you're close by, but they charged me an arm and a leg and were so unfriendly that I went to your competition afterward. It was clear they didn't want us as clients. So, your competition took over all your sport horse customers and the farmers. And they are really nice vets, too."

"That explains it. Where is that clinic?"

"Just ten kilometers up the road from here. Maybe you can visit them and have a chat, in case you need another job one day. Doesn't hurt to be on good terms with them."

"So, why do you think Michael, our vet, was killed then? Any rumors about that? Women problems?"

"No, not in town or around here. I know who is hooked up with whom, even the secret ones, but I haven't heard anyone talk about him having annoyed any husband or father of a girl. It must have to do something with the racehorses because he was so friendly with Alan from the training stables. They were close buddies."

"I guess I'll find out soon enough," I say and pick up my box of shopping.

"I wouldn't if I were you. There is a bit of gossip about race fixing going around, but they haven't been pulled up by the racing stewards ever. So, it's either not true, or they're in on it, too. Keep to yourself until you know your way around here and the people you're dealing with. This bit of advice has served me well over the years."

"Yeah, that's what Michael said to me, too, on my first day here. Maybe I'll come back some other day to talk to you about the more ancient history of this area. I'm interested in what it was like here a hundred years ago."

"Sure. I'm not really from this area, but I know who you need to ask. There are some people who have asked me questions like that in the past."

I wonder who the people are who showed interest in the past. I think she's keen to talk and gossip because the supermarket isn't busy and her only form of entertainment during working hours is talking to the customers.

On the way back to the cottage, I think about what I heard. At least the mystery of the dearth of horse patients is solved, and I know that Alan and Mike were friends, even though Alan didn't show any sign of feeling sad about his friend's demise. There are rumors and I now have been warned more than once to keep my nose out of the hospital's business with the trainers.

Parking my SUV at the front door to unpack, Precious welcomes me from the doormat.

"Mmmmrrowmmow," she says, a juvenile rabbit draped over her fangs. The rabbit's hind feet touch the ground on the left side, and its seemingly lifeless nose and ears touch the wooden floor on the right side. She drops the rabbit at my feet, calmly watching me as it sits up and looks around for an escape, frozen in fear.

"I know where you got it from. But why did you get it, Precious? You know I don't eat rabbits."

Then I realize. She wants to give me a hint about something to do with the warren in the maze.

"Okay, okay, Precious. I got the message. I'll discuss with Nan what to do about the phone in the rabbit warren. Thanks for reminding me."

Precious takes her gaze off the rabbit and lets it dart off into the garden bed.

While I unpack the car with George mingling around my feet to find out whether I brought anything interesting for him to eat, Nan's phone neighs in my back pocket.

"Hi Nan, can I put you on speaker? I am busy stocking my pantry and freezer."

"Sure. What did you find out since we talked last?"

"Lots, Nan, lots."

"Yes?" she says, and from her voice, I can hear that she is impatient. If she were real, she would grab me by the shoulders and stare right into my eyes to make me speak faster,"

"Michael got killed by an injection of horse tranquilizers."

"Oh my, that makes sense. He was a vet, after all, and had access to them."

"But he didn't kill himself. Someone else injected him, and that someone knew what they were doing."

"They could have used his own drugs, though."

That thought hadn't occurred to me. "I wonder if the Chief Conductor also checked the Raptor for missing drugs."

"They have," says Nan.

"How do you know that, Nan?"

"I know because I'm a ghost and can go anywhere, with some limitations. I mean within the boundaries. And I have my connections."

"Which boundaries, Nan? The cottage and the vet clinic or the boundaries of the property?"

"Yes, the boundaries of the property. If you look at the map, you can see them clearly marked."

"But Nan, the map is from 1920. The boundaries are out of date now."

"No, they are not out of date for me. You should be glad, too, because I can keep my eyes on you easier than with these newfangled Google maps."

"Your ghost eyes, Nan. I hope they can see in the dark. Speaking of the dark, we need to talk about the boundaries and this property later, once this case is solved; because you and Mum have kept me in the dark for so long about it."

"No point in getting snitchy, Riona. What else did you find out?"

"Michael didn't have any women problems in the area here as far as the town gossip goes, so his death has nothing to do with a disgruntled husband lashing out at him."

"But it could have been one of the clinic vets? Or he could have had an affair with Olga, Leonard's wife."

"I don't think so. Although he lived in Leonard's mansion, that's possible. Leonard would be strong enough to inject Michael and put him on the operating table."

"Another line of inquiry, Riona."

"Are you suggesting I should check out Michael's room in the mansion now?"

"He didn't have only one room. He had a flat upstairs with a separate entrance. You could check."

"This is just too scary, Nan. Maybe not tonight. I couldn't see the entrance the other night and need to scout out the place first before I do that in earnest."

"What else did the supermarket lady say. Her name is Rebecca, by the way. She is ok and you can rely on her to be honest."

"She said there are rumors about Michael and Alan from the training stable being close buddies and that there are rumors about race fixing or doping and such things. She warned me that this is a dangerous topic to ask about."

"I agree. Race fixing is usually done for money, and those people are usually dangerous, too. There would be lots of money involved to make them kill someone."

"There's also Michel's phone, Nan. I know it's in the rabbit warren, but why is it there, and why didn't the murderer leave it with Michael?"

"Maybe he called or texted the killer, and they had to get rid of it. A rabbit warren is a good pace because it's all underground."

"Precious reminded me a few minutes ago to do something about it. There must be something on the phone that is useful for the police. Otherwise, Precious wouldn't be so persistent about the warren."

Nan lets out a long sigh, a ghost snort of some kind. It sounds like a watered-down version of Princess' warning snorts.

"For the time being, just stay away from asking questions. Do your research on their racehorses, their jockeys, and the staff, tonight, before you even think of going there."

"I will, Nan. Maybe the Chief Conductor is already looking into them. Hopefully, because that would save me the effort."

"Chief Conductor?"

"Chief Inspector Brown. I call him Chief Conductor because it makes him squirm and because he looks like our school orchestra conductor."

Nan lets out a ghostly giggle that makes the glasses in the kitchen cupboard chirp.

"Have you heard from your man down the hill?"

"What man, Nan?" I pretend I don't know what she means.

"Your charmer farmer boy next door."

"He's not a boy, and I haven't heard from him. If I keep George at my place, there is no reason for me to talk to him until he feels like coming up for a chat about something to do with long grass."

Nan giggles again as if that had been a great joke.

"But he might know more about this than you think, Riona. His family has lived here a very long time."

"Nan, spit it out. If you know something helpful, please share it with me. It might keep me from stepping into some evil mess that I would rather avoid."

"It's not important now for this case, Riona. But he might also have a few bales of hay for Princess."

"Maybe you should give him a ghostly tap on the shoulder to roll a few hay bales up the hill, Nan. I need to go now because my after-hours shift starts soon. Nite Nite, Nan."

"Keep your twitch close by; you might need it."

"Grrrr-anny, I need to go."

But before I do, I hide the blood results sheets in one of Nan's poisonous plant diaries in the small room and push the green trunk back to conceal the existence of the hidden door.

Chapter 27

In some way, I feel relieved that I probably won't need to expect any random horse owner to appear tonight. They will go to the other vet clinic, our competition. That will give me time to do my research.

The clinic is deserted; everyone has gone home; I hear the pigeons' hard feet clicking on the tin roof above reception, unhurriedly cooing and fluttering off every now and then. It's still daylight. I take my sandwich and sit down on a rock next to the stallion's yard. From there, I can see that the maze hedge is far longer than I had appreciated the other night.

I want to befriend the stallion so he doesn't spook every time I come past his yard. I hold out a hand, but he ignores me and walks off to his hay net. I talk to him, telling him about Princess and that she had been Nan's horse, about my accident and that I haven't been game enough to get back on a horse since. I try to flatter him by telling him that riding him would be a dream for any rider. He just snorts in disgust as if a fly had entered his nostrils and needed to be expelled.

Maybe he is also a familiar who can understand people, but whose familiar would he be? Leonard's? That
would mean that Leonard is a male witch. What do you
call a male witch? Or was the stallion Michael's horse?
Michael never said he had a horse or wanted one. Or
maybe Barracuda is Olga's familiar. I need to learn more
about her. Who is she, and where does she come from?
Who else lives in the mansion? And what happens in the
building next to the mansion.

"Hi, Barracuda. Are you a familiar of someone here? If
yes, please let me know and I will talk with Nan about it.
She knows everyone and all the familiars here, too."

I feel a little silly talking to the stallion and don't really
expect him to give me a clear hint or a sign that acknowl-
edges his connection to the paranormal world, but all he
does is turn his backside to me and lower his head as if
what I said was not worthy of his attention.

The hedge past the stallion yard doesn't look as tall
in daylight as at night. It stretches for at least half a
kilometer in a straight line. Walking past the stallion yard
for about a hundred meters, I'm blocked from following
to its end by a six-strand sheep fence with an electric
outrigger on the other side. There is a small band of
horses in a paddock further down toward another road
on which I see cars. That road must be the highway by
which I arrived. I need to check on Google Maps to

see if there is another separate entrance to the property from that road. That would have made it possible for the murderer to escape if he or she arrived from there and left the same way.

Back at the hospital, I make myself a cup of tea in the staff room and sit down in Amy's comfortable office chair. To my surprise, Precious rests in the in-tray—or is it the out-tray? She looks like a bread loaf, paws tucked under, purring softly, and blinking at me as I log onto the computer.

"How did you get in here, Precious?"

She winks, and her mouth gives me a little oblique grin. I should know better than to ask a familiar about her trade.

What to research first? Maybe the vet clinic website. It looks cheerful and professional but only gives the most basic information about services and the contact details are the main phone number. There is a Google map to find your way there, but no details about any of the staff. This means there is no need to update the website if a vet leaves and a new one starts. It doesn't even say who owns the hospital.

How can I find out more? Then, I see it at the bottom of the home page. There is the copyright *Green Bowlder Pty Ltd.* At least, that's something.

I follow the internet breadcrumbs to an investment company that owns several other companies involved in land development, horse breeding, and racehorse training worldwide. Under the investors involved in horse breeding and training establishments, I find our vet hospital and the racing stable. Interesting.

"Wow," I say to Precious, who looks at me as if I'm a little dim and should have been aware of that a long time ago.

"Let's see who the people are who own and manage this Green Bowlder outfit

It appears that Leonard is on the board of directors of the company, but there are others whose names I have never heard.

I spend another hour digging deeper into this hornet's nest of websites, and luckily, my photographic memory helps me store all this information in my brain.

After what feels like ages, I think I have nailed down the flow of investments in this enterprise. It seems that the horse businesses, including the vet clinic, are owned by businesses that invest in gambling and property development.

The whole spiderweb leads to London and Hong Kong. The main investor, a so-called philanthropist, is a Citizen of the Russian Federation, a Mr. Fyodor Vladimir Baryshnikov.

Baryshnikov is a very rich man, an oligarch, if you were to judge by the possessions he has accumulated in his life. A mega yacht, a football club in Italy, a baseball team in the USA, and investments in the Cayman Islands. He apparently lives in London.

And what about Hong Kong? Maybe Lei is involved. He is from Hong Kong. Why did he want me to introduce him to Alan? Was that just for show, or is this another clue I need to follow? I better be careful around him.

"Oh my," I hear a whisper in my right ear.

"Nan? What are you doing here? You give me the fright of my life every time you turn up without warning."

My heart gallops in my chest. I look around but can't see Nan.

"Nan, I think I'll call you 'Ghostie' from now. I wish I could see you, so I'm forewarned that you're around here somewhere before you start talking to me."

Ghostie ignores my comment.

"That's bad news, Riona, mega bad news." Her voice comes now from the other end of the reception counter near the entrance door.

"Why is that bad news? It is what it is. Leonard is involved with people in the gambling industry and in property development. But what does this have to do with Michael's death?"

"What is bad is that it all goes back to London and Russia. d. Svetlana's curse is well and truly working and now her tentacles have reached here." Nan's voice sounds jittery and fearful.

"Who's Svetlana?"

"My mother's sister. Remember? You read the article in the 'Paranormal Monthly. She was the twin sister of Elena and cursed my mother's family."

"But this was ages ago, Nan. And who says that Michael died because he had a connection to your mother's family? He did not. Michael came from Cootamundra and that is so far from Russia you wouldn't even find it on a world map at the time when your aunt cursed your mum. Be realistic, Ghostie."

"I am very realistic, Riona. You need to learn how to protect yourself from curses and learn some basic witchcraft skills."

"Nan, I am a vet, and believe in science, not witchcraft. The time of witches has passed. At least in vet science."

"No, it hasn't. I can almost guarantee you that what happened here is all because of the consequences of Svetlana's curse."

"Almost, Nan, but you're not completely sure."

"Well, it won't hurt to be more careful so you don't meet the same end as Michael."

Before I can answer, Nan's phone neighs next to Precious. She turns into a fur ball, hackles all over her body, and her eyes are black and angry.

She hadn't worried about Ghostie popping up next to me and arguing, but now she is on high alert.

"Who did you give my number to?" asks Nan. I can hear the fear in her voice.

"Yees?" I draw out the word as long as possible without making it sound ridiculous.

"Riona, is this you? I just wanted to check whether this number works. It's Alan here. Nothing to worry about. I just wanted to check whether you are contactable on that number."

"Of course, it works. I wouldn't have given it to you if it didn't work. Do you have an emergency with a horse? I hope you have a truck or a float to bring it in. Even though I'm on call, I think it would be better to bring it in here because Leonard could help, in case I need it."

"No, no emergency. I just wanted to check whether the phone really works. I have the number now in my phone contact register for future use. We are now connected, if you know what I mean."

"I think I understand what you mean. I need to go, Alan. I have work to do. Bye-bye."

I hang up before he can answer.

Was this call just to have my details in his phone or to make sure any checking of his or my phone would show up as a call?

"Nan, are you here?" I call out.

"Yes, I'm here," she whispers. "I don't trust this man."

"Neither do I, Nan. I think both Nerida and Michael were involved in something with the racing stables that is not above board. But I'm not sure if Leonard would have known about it. It must have something to do with the racehorses and the blood samples."

"Or with the oligarch. Do you think Nerida and Michael worked together?"

"No, I don't think so because she dropped off something at the stables the same day Michael and I went there for blood samples. That could have been done in the same visit."

"What did Nerida drop off there?"

"I don't know. Let me check in the pharmacy to see if these tubs are in there or if they came from somewhere else."

I fully expect the pharmacy to be locked but it's not. The shelves are stocked to the brim with all kinds of drugs, antibiotics, worm pastes, feed additives, bandages, surgery materials, and boxes with saline solution. But I cannot find anything that resembles these white tubs with blue lids.

This is another mystery that I promise to solve. I remember that Nerida came out of the hospital with the box to load it into the car. Maybe Leonard had given it to her. He gave me a similar box of electrolytes to drop off for Alan. Maybe the shed is used for making drugs and other stuff for racehorses. That seems to be the most logical use.

"Nan, what do you think about me checking out the shed near the mansion? I want to see what they do there. It's dark now, and I can go through the maze."

"No, Riona, not today. You don't know enough about Leonard yet. He may be much more involved with the Russians than you think. They are not to be trifled with, and they'd have no problem killing you on the spot if any of them were there working for Leonard. Google him first."

It's almost midnight now, but I start another search, this time on Leonard. Fortunately, there is no shortage of pictures of him from his university days and his positions at Sydney University. LinkedIn shows me his CV, with a few of Leonard's business involvements; it's all quite professional and conventional looking.

One of his achievements is the invention of a natural electrolyte race recovery feed additive for racehorses. The company that manufactures it is listed at 1436 Green Bowlder Highway in Green Bowlders.

That's here. I think he makes this in the shed, and this is what Nerida dropped off. Maybe Nerida is actually employed by Leonard to distribute that stuff.

My head spins, but I know that all this information will sort itself out in my brain if I get a few hours of sleep.

"Time to log off, Precious," I say, as I grab my twitch next to the keyboard, and Precious gets up out of her in-tray.

"Just make sure you erase your browsing history before you log off," says Nan.

"Thank you, Nan. How could I not think about that?"

Chapter 28

I jolt up from the noise of the roller door and dash out to see who has entered the stables. Precious had been sleeping against my stomach, cuddling up, and is now off to catch her breakfast. It's seven in the morning.

Lorna is looking into each box hoping for a patient that might have come in during the night.

"I must disappoint you, Lorna. I wish we had more patients."

She checks the whiteboard that tells stable staff what to feed any new patient, just in case. Leonard has written a message in red on it.

'Stomach ulcer day! Six horses coming in at 8 o'clock.'

He must have come in early because that message was not there when I bunked down on the sofa.

"Lorna, I need to run home to get some brekkie and brush my teeth. I'll be back in a minute."

Running like the clappers, I quickly feed Princess her cup of pellets and give George a sniff-around outside his run.

"I'll ask Rocky to bring us some hay later."

Putting the kettle on and making a sunny side up egg for my toast, I think back to my computer searches yesterday. I am convinced that Leonard, Nerida, and Michael - and possibly Lei - are involved in something fishy at the racing stable. Probably, they had a disagreement, and Michael was killed by one of them.

Today, Elena's expression seems to tell me that she isn't sure my thoughts have been thoroughly sorted through. Maybe my conclusions need some rework.

"It's okay, Great-Grandma. I won't draw any rushed conclusions.

George desperately wants to come with me to the hospital.

"Not today, George, sorry. I'll ask Rocky to give you some work while I am out so you aren't so bored."

When I arrive at the hospital, I take the time to admire the horses that have arrived in a shiny blue truck with the logo of the training stables.

"At last, horses!" I whisper.

I'm excited to see a few horses and watch as Alan and his helper lead them to their stalls in the stable to wait for their examinations.

Leonard immediately asks me to fetch the endoscope from the instrument room.

He shows me how to set it up, and then Alan leads out the first horse, a suspicious two-year old chestnut horse with three white socks.

"Riona, twitch him if you don't mind, so he stands still when I insert the stomach tube for the endoscope."

Approaching the horse as if I were his best friend, I speak soothingly to him.

"Hi there, sorry, mate. I'm going to put the twitch on you so it doesn't annoy you so much when we put this tube in your nose."

I slip the twitch loop over his upper lip before he realizes what happened and twist the handle, not quickly enough to spook the horse, but in a steady, firm movement. He gives me a surprised look, but relaxes. The twitch handle feels warm and sends a subtle buzz from my fist to his body.

"Wow! That went better than I expected," says Alan.

"What did you expect?"

Leonard laughs and inserts the stomach tube and the endoscope, and in no time, we have a view on the computer screen of the horse's stomach lining. Leonard moves the scope around to examine the horse.

"You're right, Alan; he does have ulcers, but he should be fine once we put him on my special treatment."

"Pffft!" That is Ghostie again, whispering into my right ear. She appears to be floating between me and the horse's shoulder. I barely catch myself before calling out to her to disappear and not embarrass me.

"I could have told you he had ulcers right from the way he walked in. But it is interesting to see it. It's like a magic wand full of electricity to make pictures on computers. Wow."

I grit my teeth, focusing on not loosening my twitch.

Leonard removes the scope, and I release the loop from the horse's lip. He seems relieved that the procedure is over.

"Next," says Leonard as Alan takes the second horse from his stable hand, a nervous, dark bay filly, fidgeting and trying to creep backward into the box.

I pat her neck to calm her.

"Hi, little girl." Moving my hand up to her neck, I gently rub the twitch handle under the fine curtain of her mane. "Come on, we'll get it done quickly."

"Good work," whispers Nan.

Surprisingly, she is calmer and follows Alan's tuck on the lead rope.

"Now, use your magic wand again. It seems to calm them," he mutters.

And it does. A little comment to the young horse about how I'm going to use the twitch, and in a few minutes, she, too, is diagnosed with stomach ulcers.

"You could see that from a mile away," comments Nan. "But this one will be harder to treat because she is so fearful of everything. I think she has bad eyesight, so the world looks scary to her. Maybe one of these days, you could do an eye check for her."

I just nod, and Alan brings over his next horse. The same routine leads to all but one horse being diagnosed with ulcers.

Leonard asks Alan to wait for the medicine for the horses. When he comes back after a few minutes, he carries a box with exactly the same tubs that I saw Nerida drop off at the training stables.

"They need to stay on this treatment for a while. Let's check in a month to see how they go. If you run out, call, and Riona will drop more off at the stables.

There goes my theory of Leonard or Nerida being involved in shady drug treatments. He just makes normal medicines in the shed. I need a new theory about why Michael died.

"Where's Molly?" I ask Leonard as if her absence had just now occurred to me.

"The police kept Molly until late last night," says Leonard. "But they've finally let her go. I gave her the day off today to recover. I think they realized she would be far too disorganized to plan and pull off a murder."

"What about Nerida? Where is she?"

"Stay out of her way today. She's in a bad mood. They were apparently not very nice to her and tried to make her confess to Michael's murder."

"Why would she murder him?" says Alan. "I thought they were in love, those two. At least that's the impression I got from the way Nerida talked about him."

"He is lying," whispers Nan into my ear. I flinch as if a mosquito had bitten me and slap my thigh to pretend I swatted it.

"Maybe she was in love with him, but he wasn't in love with her," I suggest. Alan laughs as if that was a joke.

"I can't imagine how he could have allowed himself to get killed by a girl, even if she was the jealous type."

"Nerida isn't weak. She does a lot of weight lifting and gym work," says Leonard. "But I can't believe she would ever be a murderer. The police must have come to that conclusion, too; otherwise, they wouldn't have let her go. Now it's time to clean the scope and get ready for outside calls, Riona. Any questions about stomach ulcers?"

I shake my head and gather the scope to take it back into the instrument room for reprocessing for another day. My first proper busy day at work. I like it, even though I could have done without Ghostie's background comments. Where is she now, I wonder, realizing I'm hungry and it's lunchtime.

"I'm right here," her voice whispers next to me. "Let's go see Princess."

I walk along the path to the cottage, assuming that Nan will follow me silently. But no such luck. She decides to keep talking.

"Did you hear what he said? He called the twitch your magic wand. I think it is hilarious that an ordinary person can see what it is, but you don't, even though you are a witch."

"Are you saying that this twitch is a magic wand? What else can it do apart from twitching horses?"

"Let me show you."

We walk to Princess' stable. She nickers in the direction of my right shoulder. Can she see Nan?

"My darling Princess. I miss you so much. Let me show this little ignorant witch here how to use the twitch to calm horses without clamping it onto their lip."

I hold the twitch out toward Princess, assuming that Nan would take it.

Nan giggles her trademark silver bell laugh.

"No, you take it in both hands and rub the handle over her shoulders and back like a gentle massager. The carving will loosen any old hair. It is like a massage roller in a gym. Not that I used massage rollers in my time, but I have seen them on TV. Try it."

Princess seems to appreciate the massage, stretching and twisting her neck, her lips moving as if she were scratching another horse.

"Sometimes horses are sore because of bad saddles or poor riding, but when you use the twitch over their muscles, gently and methodically, they tell you where it hurts, and then you can give them more targeted massages."

I start from the front of Princess' neck behind the ears and work the twitch all over her body right to the top of her tail. She stands still appreciatively until we're finished, lunch all but forgotten.

I pat her one more time and clip the twitch back to my belt.

"Time for a sandwich and coffee."

"It also works on people. You can use it when you are stiff and sore. It will help you, but don't use it on yourself when others are looking. They will think you are mad."

I make myself a cheese and tomato toastie and put my feet on the little coffee table in the living room. The picture of Elena looks more relaxed now, even though I am no closer to a solution to the mystery of Michael's death.

Maybe it has nothing to do with the vet hospital at all. Maybe it has something to do with the cottage.

But first, I need to call Rocky to find out whether I can buy some hay from him.

I call his number while I sip my coffee. He answers instantly.

"Hi Rocky, I wonder if you know where I can buy a roll or two of hay – or some small bales - for Princess. And maybe a few bales of Lucerne hay for a treat. She is elderly and needs a little extra special food."

"I can bring a roll of hay over for you. Once she has eaten it, I'll bring the next. You don't have the equipment to move hay rolls. I'll get someone to drop off ten bales of lucerne hay for you next week if that is okay with you."

"That is perfect, Rocky, thanks."

An awkward silence follows because I don't know how to keep the conversation going. We're casual acquaintances, after all, even though I'm fascinated by his eyes and his calmness.

"Any news about the police and you being a suspect? I hope you're in the clear now," he says.

"Nerida and Molly were suspected too, but were released. Any suspicions I had over Leonard being involved have also been cleared up."

"No, I don't think he would ruin his business by murdering his own staff. But Nerida, I wouldn't put it past her. I heard her and Michael argue and fight all the time when he lived in the cottage. I could hear them screaming at each other when I was mustering cows or sheep next to the cottage."

"What did they fight about?"

"I don't know. Maybe lovers' disagreements. Who knows? It didn't sound pleasant, but she always came back for more. She could have stayed away from him, but she kept visiting—not every day, but most days. Until he moved into the mansion."

"Let's talk about it when you bring the hay."

"How about tomorrow after work? Can you please warn Leonard that I'll be driving through with the hay? He normally doesn't like me coming to the place, so it's better he knows and stays in his mansion."

He laughs and hangs up. I cannot stop smiling. Have I been missing Rocky? No, I haven't, I tell myself. Fortunately, Ghostie must be busy on the other side because she would have surely had a comment about that.

This means that Nerida is still a suspect, but I'll find out more tomorrow. I wonder if Molly will be back then, and where Lei was this morning?

Chapter 29

T he phone next to my head neighs, waking me up. There is no picture or number displayed on its screen.

"Yes, Nan, how is your morning?" I say as I stretch under the quilt.

"Don't be ridiculous, Riona. Every day is the same here. If I don't find my own entertainment, it gets really boring. How did you do last night? Precious told me she is trying to entice you to do something about the phone?"

"Nan, it's a bit scary to follow a cat into a hedge at night. The dogs could attack us. Didn't you tell me to wait until I know more?"

"I know, I know, but I thought you wouldn't listen because the dogs didn't attack you last time. I don't understand why you didn't bring the phone home then. I'd like to know what is on it."

"Nan, I left it because I couldn't reach it, and I couldn't think straight after the dogs chased us, and Precious screamed. We need to tell the police where it is."

"But they'll think you put it there. You need to come up with a better idea than that."

"Maybe I could send a message from Michael's phone to a few suspects and see who turns up in the maze to get it back. The killer either lost it in the rabbit warren or has hidden it there on purpose. If they get a message from it, they'll get a real shock and realize that someone knows where it was dumped."

"Hmm, I think it would be better if you could give the Chief Inspector the idea that he hasn't searched every last spot on the place. Give him a few breadcrumbs to follow so he thinks it was all his idea."

"Maybe I could give him a call to get my phone back and ask him if they searched Leonard's mansion and gardens for electronics. I could mention that I had seen the cat disappearing into the hedge a few times and come out with toys."

"That sounds like something you could try."

"Or you could appear in his dreams and whisper in his ear to search the hedge like you whisper into my ear to wake up."

"I could do that too, but he doesn't live close by. I know he lives somewhere close to Green Bowlders township, which is actually almost too far from his real job in the big smoke. But he likes the area and takes the daily commute instead of moving away from here."

"I'll ask Rocky where he lives exactly. He knows everyone in Green Bowlders."

"Ah, yes, your new boyfriend, Rocky. Is he selling you some hay?"

"Yes, Nan, he'll be bringing a hay roll over this evening after work. As if you didn't know."

"I'll be there to meet him in person."

"Please, Nan, don't appear as a full-blown Ghost. Not that it would matter if he'd get cold feet talking to me, but I want to keep in the good books with the neighbors. Please, don't meddle."

Nan giggles her little laugh into my ear.

"I think I'll show him the map in the little room. He seems to be up to date about the area and has a bit of knowledge about the history, too. I want to find out if there is another way into the hospital than from the road and from Leonard's place. I'll check if the hedge and the maze are drawn on the map."

"The maze was here when my mother and Friederike moved here with me. I can remember it clearly, but it wasn't very tall then, and fell into disrepair after I grew up. It was so hard to keep up the hedge and the grass in the maze. I think Leonard doesn't even know there is a maze. He probably thinks it's just a hedge."

"Nan, I need to feed Princess and go to work. I'll talk to you when I get back home."

I brew myself a large mug of coffee and pull a couple of fillet steaks out of the freezer to defrost. They'll be just right for grilling, and maybe Rocky will have one of them.

I wonder what work might bring today. Hopefully, a few horses with something interesting to investigate. Not that I wish any horse to suffer an injury, but I would like to practice my stitch up skills.

And then there is Nerida. How am I going to approach her? If the Chief Conductor has interviewed her, would he have grilled her the same way he grilled me? Would she be a tougher nut to crack? She is older than me, maybe eight or ten years, fit and strong, and doesn't like being upstaged by anyone. I don't like the silly laughs at the end of her sentences, but would she have kept that up in a police interview? I wonder whether Chief Inspector Brown has taken her phone, too. I'll start by asking Nerida that question.

Princess nuzzles my ponytail, and I stroke her face, tracing the half-moon-shaped scar with my right thumb. I wonder how and when she got it.

Filling her hay net with the last hay I had brought with me, I tell her, "Today you get new hay, Princess."

Chapter 29

Nerida is chatting with Amy in reception when I arrive. Her silly laugh on the other side of the door makes my mood drop a couple of octaves. My shoulders tense, and my teeth clench together.

"Hi, Amy," I make a point of greeting her first to avoid Nerida's silly laugh a little longer. "Is Molly back today?"

"Yes, she is, but she's out on a call."

"Hi Nerida, how are you? Did the Chief Inspector interview you too? You must have been able to get him off your back; otherwise, you wouldn't be here now."

"I sure did get him off my back; there was nothing he could hold me for, hehehe."

"Did he take your phone, too? He's still got mine. I have to get it back because I need it to talk to clients and call my family."

"Yes, he took my phone, but it won't be any good for him. I don't keep any messages that I get. I delete everything the minute I read it, hehehe."

"Really? Even the work texts and emails?"

"I keep nothing private. Private is private, and I delete it immediately, hehehe."

I spin one of Amy's biros in a circle on the counter to focus my mind and distract Nerida.

"Wow, I have never met anyone who does that. But how do you know something work-related doesn't turn into something private? Like working with Michael turning into something private with him?"

I see Amy's fingers hover in slow motion over her keyboard, her body frozen in her chair.

"I didn't have anything private with Michael, hehehe."

"And if you did, you would have deleted it, wouldn't you?"

"I would, but that is not any concern of yours, hehehe."

"You know what the Chief Inspector said to me when he took my phone?"

"What did he say?"

"He said that nowadays, they can resurrect all deleted messages in their forensic IT laboratory. I think he said that just to scare me, though."

That was pure invention, made up on the spot just to see Nerida's reaction to the possibility of her deleted messages being found. A microsecond of fear crosses her face and lingers in her eyes. *Gotcha. You do have something to hide.*

"He won't find anything on my phone," she says, this time without adding her little laugh, and turns toward the stables. Amy resumes her typing and looks up at me.

"What was that about?"

"A few people have told me that she had a relationship with Michael. And now she says she deleted all private messages from her phone? Really? It's very strange."

"But everyone knows about their relationship—if you could call it a relationship. It was more like war and peace with nobody winning."

"Then it's even stranger that she thinks the police believe her story that there was no private connection with Michael."

"Maybe her connection with him had to do with them being vets? They were both super jealous about who brought more money into the clinic each month."

"No, I don't think so. They would have enjoyed that competition forever and a day. It must have been something different that got Michael killed. He told me to keep out of things that didn't concern me when I first arrived."

Amy's face takes on a vague and distant expression as if she went through a mental list of potential shortcomings or professional complaints of Michael's actions over the years.

"I can't imagine anything here that would get him killed," she says eventually.

"Maybe it had to do with his favorite racehorse trainers. Or the Botox receptionist, Rose."

Amy burst out laughing.

"Botox Rose? Her? She is the dumbest nitwit in the shire. She thinks pumping herself up with fillers can cover up the absence of brain cells. She wouldn't be able to pull off anything illegal with Michael, and he wouldn't have used her as an accomplice because she is so stupid."

"Maybe he trod on her boyfriend's toes by dating her?"

"She doesn't have a boyfriend. She never has more than one date with anyone, but she's had many dates."

Now, it's my turn to laugh, but a client entering reception interrupts me. At last, a horse. I go to the breezeway to check that the crush is clean, even though I know it had been cleaned yesterday afternoon.

After a few minutes, the horse and its owner enter the breezeway at the same time as Leonard.

"Riona, now that Michael is no longer with us, you need to learn how we desex young horses. You'll be my assistant today, and from then on, you need to get the surgery done in the field on your own. We only have older stallions come in for desexing in the hospital. The young'uns will be part of your outside visits."

My mind focuses quickly and after a few minutes, the young colt has lost his future career as a breeding stallion. I'm ready to help more of these youngsters start a more temperate existence as geldings. Leonard is happy with my assistance and tells me that I'm ready to be Michael's replacement, for the time being.

Thinking about asking what Michael had meant when he'd warned me to keep my nose out of the hospital's business, it seems safer not to right now. I'll discuss it with Ghostie first. She probably knows more about Leonard than I do. All I know is that Leonard is involved in property development with the Russian oligarch. How would Michael fit into that?

"Have they found Michael's phone?" I ask instead.

"Not that I've heard. They searched his flat, but the dog found nothing except his computer, his race car seat, and the app for the TV."

"Car racing?"

"Yes, he practiced it virtually, Formula One and off-road races."

"I had no idea that he liked stuff like that. But racing his Raptor in the outback somewhere was probably his dream. He was so proud of the Raptor and told me how much he paid. How did he get the money for it, I wonder."

"Keep wondering because he didn't tell me either."

"Where is Lei?" I ask.

"That I don't know either."

Chapter 30

Leonard leaves me to supervise the recovery of the newly minted gelding and the cleaning of the instruments, after which it's home for lunch and a chat with Nan. But before I leave, I decide to check in the lab for any new racehorse blood samples. Maybe Nerida has been at the training stables this morning.

But there are none. I'm disappointed but wonder what other clues I might find here.

A shelf on the wall with user manuals for all the tools and processing machines that the clinic owns catches my eye. There will be no clues there, but I need to become familiar with all of them if I'm to be Michael's replacement, 'for now'. I start with one of the blood analyzers and learn how it works, and what blood criteria it can analyze.

While I read and compare its graphs and the buttons and displays of the machine, Nerida walks in and starts rummaging through the wastepaper basket.

"What's up? Lost something?" I ask in my friendliest voice.

"No, just looking for a few papers that I threw out a couple of days ago. I need to check up on something."

"What papers? I think the girls emptied the basket yesterday afternoon. They should be in the recycle bin. If it's results, wouldn't they be stored in the analyzer memory?"

"No, I always delete everything after it is finished, hahaha."

"Like your phone," I say, wanting to copy her silly laugh but stopping myself. "What's so important that you need to go back through the results? Maybe just take another sample if it's from the training stable."

Nerida rushes outside, and I put the manual back on the shelf.

Sneaking outside, I see her rummaging through the recycle bin. Time to go home. I need to have a proper look at the test sheets. What tests did she do, and what horses were important on these sheets?

Putting a cheese, ham, and tomato sandwich into my toastie maker, I pick up my phone to call Nan, suddenly wondering what number to call. Can I call the number on this phone, and she will answer? Or is there a ghost phone directory? I try Nan's phone number first and sure enough, she picks up without the phone even ringing.

"Riona darling, so nice to hear your voice. You sound so happy today."

"Nan, I haven't said anything yet."

"But I know from how the phone feels in your hand that you are much happier now than the last time I talked to you."

"True," I say while watching the cheese bubble out of the Toastie maker. "I've found out that Michael and Nerida had a relationship that was tumultuous, but I don't know how to figure out whether it had anything to do with Michael's murder. And apparently the police are still looking for Michael's phone. And Nerida is looking for the blood sample analysis sheets from days ago. Why?"

"They have to do with why Michel was murdered, of course. So, I suggest you hide them well because they will be evidence someday."

"I need to read them again first. I read them before, but I only memorized the horses, not the results."

"Then do that while you eat your toastie. I haven't had one of those for ages. It smells delicious."

After retrieving the sheets from the hidden room, I place the toastie on a plate and take it into the living room. I love the way the melted cheese stretches when it's hot.

I straighten the crunched-up papers and lay them out on the coffee table. There are six of them, giving the usual blood parameters we were taught to interpret at vet school. I stare at them and try to make sense of them. Do they show anything untoward? I need to dig out my books tonight and read more about performance-enhancing drugs. Maybe consulting Google Scholar can help.

The seventh paper is a printout from a mass spectrometer.

"Wow, Nan, they have a mass spectrometer in the lab. They are really expensive machines. Why do they have that, I wonder. I need to look at it when I get back after lunch. Maybe it's for research."

I munch my toastie faster than its delicious contents justify.

"What do we do about Michael's phone, Nan? Can't you just woosh over to it and send a text to the Chief Conductor so he comes with his dog and finds it?"

"I'll see what I can do. I am a witch, after all, albeit a ghostly one. It shouldn't be too hard."

"You're the best, Ghostie. Don't forget to be back when Rocky comes this afternoon."

"Riona, before you go back to your hospital, hide these papers really well. They are important, and someone might want them back desperately."

"Where should I put them? In the little room? Under the floorboards in the kitchen? Or on the back of Elena's painting?"

"If I were a thief, I would look at the painting first. I think the little room is safer. They won't find it behind the paneling."

I quickly scan the pages in one of Nan's poisonous plant manuals. It would be hard to find, I think. Carefully, I close the door and push the green trunk against it. Precious jumps on it, watching what I am doing. She shows absolutely no interest in the crumbs and cheesy bits of my toastie."

"Precious, make sure nobody goes in there or even looks at it." I think Nan is a little over anxious about someone trying to find papers in my cottage, but better safe than sorry.

She blinks once and I give her a quick scratch under the chin before putting my plate into the sink. George reluctantly slinks back into his dog run, and I run to the hospital.

"See you later, Princess."

In reception, I find Amy googling holiday destinations for her planned leave in a couple of months. Obviously, nothing else to do for the rest of the day.

"Anything for me?" I ask as if I was bursting out of my seams in expectation of a difficult case turning up.

"No, but you are booked in for tomorrow at the training stables for more blood samples. They want them done before the picnic races on the weekend."

"What picnic races?"

"The Green Bowlder Picnic Meet. Didn't you know?"

"Never heard of them. Okay, I'll go out there first thing in the morning. Did they say what they want analyzed?"

"No. They said just the usual."

Good time for me to check out the mass spectrometer. I don't even know what one looks like. I go from gadget to gadget in the lab and find it at the end of the bench, furthest away from the door. It doesn't look big or impressive, and I have no idea how it works. Where is its manual? On the shelf, of course. I open it up and immediately realize it assumes a lot of knowledge about its fancy words and graphs. Phew. This is going right over my head. I put the manual back on the shelf.

The machines just sit there on the bench without giving me a hint. What do I do now? I may as well get familiar with the anesthetic machine. Sooner or later, Leonard will ask me to be the one to anesthetize a horse on the operating table. But where is the manual? It's definitely not on the shelf. It might not have come with a manual if Leonard had bought a used machine. I can't find it in the operating theater either. The anesthetic machine isn't back yet from forensics. Maybe they took the manual with the machine.

Sorting through the manuals on the shelf, I'm confident I'll be able to operate all the machines and microscopes except the mass spectrometer. Maybe I need to ask Leonard or Nerida how it works. First, though, I'll ask Lei because he and Janice just walked in after a dog consult.

"Hey, Lei, do you know how the mass spectrometer works and what it's used for?"

He gives me a look of complete incomprehension. Or is it apprehension?

"We are not allowed to touch that. Only Leonard and Nerida know how to use it. Maybe you can ask them to teach you how it works."

"I'll ask Leonard tomorrow."

"He is away until next week. But I have never seen him use it, so he might have just bought it for Nerida. I think she uses it for her research."

"What research is that?"

"Racehorse performance. But she never talks about it with us. She doesn't want our help, especially not mine."

"Why not, especially yours? She hasn't asked me either."

"She says it's secret, and because I am from Hong Kong, I am not allowed to know."

I snort in laughter. "I can't believe that. Are you serious?"

"Completely serious. I think I will not renew my contract for next year here. I don't learn anything new anymore now. I must find a better place to advance my career at home."

"Good luck, Lei. Maybe in the meantime, you can help me with things I should know in case I make a silly mistake, which I sometimes am prone to."

Lei gives me the thumbs-up before walking out.

"And, Lei, there is always the competition up the road. They may have more interesting work than we have, even though they don't have the racehorses."

Chapter 31

The sun is an hour away from disappearing behind the trees. Time to take Princess' feed bin out of her paddock to allow Rocky to drive in and out without obstacles in the way.

In the tack room, I wipe the dust off the saddle on its saddle rack. It's not my saddle, but I don't want it to look neglected. Another visual scan satisfies me that the room looks inviting and professional.

I let George out of his run and fill his bowl with fresh water.

In the kitchen, I quickly wash my breakfast cup and plate and put them away. Everything looks tidy enough for a visitor. I move the standup lamp in the living room a little to the side so it better shows off its ornate, old-fashioned lampshade. I fluff up the sofa cushions; they're old and a little dusty and brittle, but they're a perfect match for the green fabric of the sofa.

In the bathroom, I take my hair tie off and brush my ponytail until all kinks and waves have turned into a clean waterfall of fine blond strands. Should I leave my hair down or tie it up again?

Better to tie it up because it's just a casual farm-related visit, not a date. My collection of scrunchies is not large but I find one with flamboyant red flowers and tie my 'Clydesdale tail' into a low ponytail at the base of my neck.

Now it's just time to wait until Rocky arrives.

George's barking alerts me to Rocky's arrival. He greets the Nissan with the big hay roll on the back with enthusiasm and circles around the slowing car.

"He's here!" whispers Nan over my shoulder. I imagine her clapping her ghostly hands, which are still invisible to me. She has promised me that, with my witches skills increasing, I will soon be able to see her. That's one good reason for studying witchcraft, even though I can't imagine any other one.

"Nan, please keep quiet and don't distract me."

"I promise. How exciting!"

I greet Rocky before he reaches the round garden bed.

"Hi, Riona, nice to see you. Where do you want it?" he says.

I point to the gate next to the stable and walk along ahead of him to open it.

Princess stands back without me having to tell her. Rocky drives through, and I shut the gate, walking through the next gate from the yard to Princess' small paddock. The mare follows the car and tries to snatch a few hay stalks from the round bale while the Nissan is still moving.

Rocky drives a circle and stops the car, nose forward to drive straight out again, and switches the engine off.

Our eyes meet, and we both smile politely. I feel I need to say something, but nothing comes to mind that wouldn't sound cheesy, so I don't say anything. What is there to say? He knows what he is doing and unfastens the rope that holds the bale in place before raising the truck bed a little to let the ball slide off to the ground.

"Perfect," I say, as it lands with a thud. Rocky cuts the bale's netting wrapper and pulls it away from the hay. I have seen people just leave the wrapping on until the horses have finished their hay.

"Thanks for taking it off. It is a little hard to do, but I prefer it off. Ready for a cup of tea?"

"Sure. Let me just drive the car out to the front of the cottage."

While he parks the Nissan, I enter through the back-door to start the kettle and open the front door right as Rocky is about to knock.

"Come in and find a seat. There are only a few to choose from."

He walks to the kitchen with me, looking around as if he's comparing it with an image he had in his mind.

"The kitchen hasn't changed since Michael lived here."

He glances out the backdoor.

George looks up at him, wondering if he should bark or not, then decides to keep quiet.

"I see they've put on a luxury kennel and dog run now. I think it was for Michael's dog, though, and not for yours.

"I think so. The dog house is a little too big for a Kelpie but would be perfect for a German Shepherd. Biscuits?"

"Sure. Is the dog allowed inside?"

"Yes, he is. You can let him in."

George squishes through the door and plops on the carpet in front of the sofa, ready for a pat.

Rocky follows him and sits down on the sofa, the obvious favorite spot for visitors.

"That picture wasn't there the last time I was here."

"I rescued it from the little room in the corner. Michael had banned her there because he said she looked evil," I call out from the kitchen as I empty a packet of Oreos onto a plate.

"Evil? I wouldn't say that. She reminds me of a sculpture in our little cemetery. She looks like that statue."

My hand stops in the air above the plate. What did he just say? I pour milk in a jug and sugar from the packet into a small bowl. Normally, I don't have sugar, and therefore no sugar bowl because of the ants. Before I can comment on Rocky's observation about Elena's picture, Nan's phone rings.

"Yes?" I answer. I know it is Nan because the screen is empty.

"Riona, don't worry about the cemetery. I'll tell you all about it later. Just enjoy your time together. He's a nice boy, that Rocky. I'll hang around with you now."

"Sure," I say and hang up.

Rocky gives me a quizzical look, which I choose to ignore.

I pour him a cup of tea and push the sugar and milk in front of him.

"What cemetery? Is there one in town? Maybe I'll have a look at this statue one day."

"No, the cemetery on our farm. Our land used to be part of the old estate, and they had a cemetery."

"That's curious. Do you know the name of that grave? Maybe you can take a photo of it one day."

"I could, but I think it is better if I take you there, and you can have a look for yourself."

Nan whispers from the armrest of the chair of the chair next to the fireplace. I ignore her, even though I know she is angry about me poking my nose into things that she wants to keep secret for now.

"That would be great, Rocky."

"Didn't you say you had a map here of the old estate? It probably has the cemetery marked on it."

Chapter 32

I open the hidden door in the wall paneling. The afternoon light is too low to decipher everything. I fumble for the light switch on the wall without success.

"Oh, no lights," I say disappointedly. Rocky pulls a black cord that hangs from the ceiling, and now the dim light of the small lightbulb reveals the details of the map.

It is the Anderson's Green Bowlder Estate as of 1920.

We both scan the map quietly for a while, then I point out the tiny dot that represents the cottage. The B. W. Cottage.

"It was called 'Blue Wren Cottage' once," I say.

But Rocky is more interested in the other features of the Green Bowlder Estate, the roads, boundaries and creeks. He pulls out his phone and opens the fire brigade's map to compare the two.

"I see," he says after a while. "There were more roads in those days than now. We now only have Green Bowlder Lane, the road that you come up to get to the vet hospital and the cottage here, and the road that became the highway on the other side of the original property. But there were originally others. Look here; this line is Cemetery Lane, which goes from the mansion to the cemetery. And then there is this lane here. It goes directly from the Green Bowlder to the cottage, and Green Bowlder Lane goes down from here to my place."

"What's the Green Bowlder? I haven't seen anything green around here."

"The Green Bowlder is a large round knob, a rocky outcrop in the state forest, North from here. You can't see it from here now because the cottage is in a ditch or a small valley that goes down to the creek. A bushfire happened before the Andersons came, leaving only the green mountain formation untouched. That's probably why they called it Green Bowlder. The trees are now much older and look more olive gray than green."

Ghostie whispers in my ear, "That's correct." I nod to both her and Rocky.

"This was a huge place once," says Rocky. "Many square kilometers. The only roads on this map that survived as public roads are Green Boulder Lane, where our house is, the road to here, and the highway. In theory, anyone can drive on Green Bowlder Lane because it's marked as a public road. I'll need to have a closer look before the next fire season to make sure it's completely and easily accessible for use."

"You mean the fire brigade?"

"Yes, or anyone else who would volunteer."

"Rocky, do you think Michael's killer could have come in here past the cottage from somewhere without me noticing that night? If they came through your place somehow."

Rocky scans the map again, longer than I think it should take him to come up with an answer.

"He or she could have come in from anywhere, but most likely either from the highway to the mansion and the hospital or past the cottage here. I don't think they would have climbed over the fence and traipsed through the paddocks or the State Forest."

"It must have been past here. That's why George and the horse went off their tree that night. He - or she - must have disturbed them."

Thinking about it made the hair on my arms stand on end. Scary!

"That's possible. Maybe they came from the Green Bowlder end of the lane. Maybe the police should check that out for tire tracks."

"Or," I say and pause. Maybe I shouldn't say it, but the answer will give me a new clue. "They could have come through from your end of the lane. You said you live at that end of Green Bowlder Lane."

"But I didn't hear anything that night, and you would have heard my dogs bark. They don't miss a thing."

"He might lie, Riona," whispers Nan fearfully. "Better be careful. He might be the killer." But then she laughs. "Only kidding, of course."

I almost answer Nan, but catch myself. She has a point. Maybe tomorrow, I'll take a photo of the map and drive up to Green Bowlder to check out the Lane from that end.

"That's true, I didn't hear your dogs that night. I can hear them from the hospital, though. I heard them bark the other night when I was on call. What are we going to do with all this knowledge now?"

"I am sure the police have an accurate map of the area and will check out the Lane from both ends." He pauses. "But thinking of it, they haven't come to check yet, and they haven't interviewed me either. Maybe I'm not a suspect even though I had an opportunity to come past here. Strange."

We keep studying the map.

"Look here," says Rocky. "There is a fence line here that separated the mansion and its garden from the northern part of the Estate. It looks like they planted a cypress grove there, or some kind of a hedge."

What he's pointing out is the hedge with the maze.

Rocky pulls up another map on his phone.

"You see? This is still here. I wonder why they divided the place up like that. Green Bowlder Lane was built just as a straight access road, but it would have been more for work, and the cottage would have been a manager's home, I think."

"Let's have another cup of tea. These mysteries are not exactly inspiring me to stay in the neighborhood. I'm here only for three months as it is. Unless they can't find a replacement for me, which is really unlikely."

"Awe," says Rocky. "That's not much time to get to know the neighbors."

"Do you want to stay for dinner? You can tell me more about the neighbors then."

"Sure, I haven't prepared anything yet at home, so I accept. "

I imagine Nan hopping up and down in excitement. It makes me smile. A ninety-something-year-old witch getting excited about watching her granddaughter having a dinner date with a local farmer who could be a killer. After all, he could have just driven or walked up from his house along Green Boulder Lane, past the cottage, and to the hospital to kill Michael.

"Fat chance," says Nan. "And how would he have known his way around the hospital, the drugs, and the anesthetic machine to create a ridiculous crime scene like that, hmm?"

"You're right, Nan," I answer in my mind. "But what if he had an accomplice in the clinic? Maybe Nerida, or

Lei, or even Leonard? Hmm? What do you have to say to that, Nan?"

I ignore her ghostly chitter-chatter and focus on making dinner in the presence of Rocky, who could be a killer. While chopping up vegetables, my stomach flutters watching him as he sits quietly on the sofa with George at his feet and Precious observing him calmly.

I wonder what he is thinking as his eyes follow the movements of my knife on the chopping board. My skin tingles under his gaze, and suddenly aware of the less-than-ample of my body, I feel the need to hide my inadequacy behind the kitchen table.

Chapter 33

A fter Rocky leaves, I close the door with a sigh. I didn't stuff up the steak or burn the veggies. We had plain water with it because I have not had a drop of alcohol since my accident. It was hard enough for my brain to adjust to an upright position without confusing it with booze.

Rocky drives off slowly, and I watch him with a sense of relief but also sadness that he left without giving me a hint whether he liked me.

"Nan, where are you?"

I don't wait for her answer, knowing full well that she has been watching us and listening in on our conversation the whole time.

"Nan, I don't think he's the killer. He doesn't know anything about tranquilizers and hasn't used a vet in years. He sells his bull calves off before they need to be turned into steers, and for calving difficulties, he uses the clinic up the road. He just doesn't want anything to do with Leonard and his vets."

"I know, I know. That's good to know," answers Nan.

"Nan, I wish I could see you. It's a bit disconcerting to just hear you and not see you. Where are you?"

"You need to learn to tune into my energy a little more, darling. With a little training, you will get better at it. Just watch Precious; where she goes and where she looks, and that's where I hover."

I sit down on the sofa opposite Elena's painting, and Precious hops up next to me for a scratch around her head.

"Nan, I think this investigation is stuck. The Chief Conductor may be great at organizing the orchestra of his own people, but I don't think he has a clue about what is going on here. There must be something on Michael's phone that the killer doesn't want us to discover. I think it was put into the rabbit warren on purpose, so it can't be pinged from a mobile phone tower. We need to get it out in the open so it can be found by the police."

"But how, Riona?"

"Nan, you could ask Precious to retrieve it from the warren so the police can ping it."

"Precious is your familiar now, Riona, so you need to negotiate with her yourself about what you want her to do."

I could have sworn that a small grin crossed Precious's face. Her whiskers vibrate for a split second before she gives me a one-eyed blink.

"I'll go to bed and think about it a little more. It would be best if the phone appeared somewhere in a public spot where everyone can see it, but nobody can secretly find and destroy it. What do you think, Nan? Nan?"

Nan doesn't answer, leaving me to continue to discuss the options with Precious.

"Or it could be placed on top of the warren, out of its underground entrance, for the police to get the ping info. I'm sure they'll be here in a flash once they get the phone's pings, and then they can find it with their dog. What do you think, Precious?"

The cat blinks again and ambles out into the kitchen for some of her cat food. She seems to enjoy it, or she might be politely acknowledging that I bought them just for her.

"I'll leave it to you, Precious; I wish you could talk to me, though. That would be much easier."

"She can talk, but she is an introvert and a bit of a silent type. Nite Nite, Riona."

Nan seemingly has ghosted off to her invisible perch somewhere. Or does she just bunk down on the sofa, or in the spare bedroom?

In the morning, I find George on the end of my bed, ready for work, which for him now means an existence in the kennel outside until I come home for lunch. Precious is nowhere to be seen, and Princess is busy with her round bale of hay, so I just call out a good morning and dash to the hospital. My hair is still wet from the shower, and my last clean pair of clean jeans clings to my legs as I walk along the brick path with my coffee mug. I wonder what Precious has organized for the phone.

A call to the Chief Conductor might help hurry the case along a little. It almost rings out, but then I hear his voice.

"Chief Inspector Brown, how can I help you?"

"Ah, I'm so glad to get you straight away. Chief Conductor. Riona here. Remember me? It's Riona Clay, in case you've forgotten.

"I haven't forgotten you. My favorite suspect." He laughs.

"Not funny, Chief Conductor. I am calling about my phone. Do you still need it? I'm a little limited with my Nan's phone, and would prefer my own for work. When can I get it back?"

"I told Nerida to let you know you can pick it up any time. We don't need it anymore."

"Oh, she must have forgotten to tell me."

"I have to come out today again, so I will bring it by."

"Why are you coming back? Am I still your suspect? I thought Nerida was your suspect now." I add a little laugh like Nerida's special giggle at the end of her sentences.

"Don't be so confident, Miss Clay. We have not solved the case yet. There are plenty more suspects and clues to be found. I'll see you out there in half an hour or so."

What other suspects does he want to talk to now? Lei, Janice, Leonard? Or Rocky? Should I let Rocky know that the Chief Conductor might be on his way to grill him?

I park the car and am surprised to see Precious in Amy's in-tray.

"Hi, Precious, what are you doing here? Haven't you a job to do?" I pat her, and she blinks at me, her purr motor in high gear. She gives me a slow blink.

"She doesn't come here often," says Amy. "She doesn't like the orange cat who lives in the hay shed. But sometimes she likes to check up on us all, don't you, little cat? Precious closes her eyes as if to say, *'Give me a break. I don't like hollow compliments.'*

"You need to go out to the trainers to get blood samples," says Amy.

"I will, the minute the Chief Inspector has left. He's on his way with my phone."

"I see. I'll call Alan that you'll be delayed."

In the small animal consult room where Janice examines the ears of an old spaniel, I wait until she's written a prescription for ear drops and sent the dog an owner on their way.

"Have the police interviewed you too? They're on their way back here. I wonder what they want," I say, hoping she volunteers a few morsels of information.

"Yes, they did talk to me, and they took my phone to get all the info off, but I got it back yesterday when I was in town. They didn't have any further comments, except that I shouldn't leave the country. Fat chance for that, considering the money here doesn't allow overseas travel, and I don't have enough holidays left in the first place."

"Maybe they want to talk to Lei instead."

"They interviewed him for about half a day. He said hey went through all of his visa details and history in Hong Kong. But they let him go. I think he doesn't have his phone back yet, considering that half of what is on it is in Chinese."

Nerida is not in the staff room and must be out on calls. Back at reception, I see that Precious is gone. I look into the horse stalls but can't see her anywhere. What has she planned? I fetch blood tubes and test sheets from the store room to be ready for the blood samples the minute the Chief Conductor is gone.

It seems the only suspect not yet interviewed is Rocky. I nervously twiddle with the twitch at my belt as the unmarked police car arrives.

Chapter 34

The Chief Inspector, his Chief Conductor hairstyle tamed into a tight man bun at the back of his neck, this time in a light gray suit and white trainers, leaps out of his car like a leopard on the hunt. He hands me my phone without a word as he talks on his own phone.

"I'll wait here for you," he says, turning his attention to the entrance gate.

"More to come?" I ask, waiting for a little more conversation. He would be so much more relatable if he weren't so arrogant, but then, I prefer the banter with an arrogant man more than with a friendly, bland one. Does this mean I like him better than Rocky? But then ... These white shoes, how can they be so white?

Before he can answer, a police car drives in and parks next to the unmarked one. And out hops the detective with his K9 companion. I smile. Precious has been at work. Let's see what happens. Show time!

"What's up, Chief Conductor?"

"I wish you wouldn't call me that, Miss Clay. We are doing another search. Michael's phone has become active again, and it sounds as if it's located on this property."

"Oh, how surprising. Do you want me to call Leonard?"

"He is interstate, and he doesn't need to be here. We have a search warrant, which I need to show the receptionist, and then we can start our search."

I lead him to Amy and then follow him out into the yard behind the hospital and toward the stallion yard where Barracuda stands in the morning sun, a glistening picture of health and power.

My heart skips a beat when I see Precious sitting in the middle of the stallion's yard, a tricolored Egyptian statue, silent, her orange eyes glowing. Next to her, in the sand, lies an object that suspiciously looks like a phone, covered in a black case. Of course, it's not black anymore, but covered in dried mud and soil, its carry loop trodden into the dirt. I'm still smiling, wondering how the police are going to retrieve it from the yard.

As we approach the stallion yard, the electronics dog starts pulling on his harness and starts yapping in the direction of Precious.

"Leave the cat alone," I say. "She doesn't have any electronics in her."

"Miss Clay, I wish you would mind your own business and let us do ours."

"No worries, Chief Conductor," I say, stepping back. How are they going to 'find' the phone, with Precious sitting there, seemingly a distraction, and the stallion who has now woken up from his absentmindedness?

The dog handler walks around the yard, and his dog barks at the phone sitting at the fence, eyeing it from the distance.

Precious makes the find easy. She walks off in slow motion, under the rails and out to me, wrapping herself around my legs, purring and tail held high. The dog still points at the spot where Precious had been sitting.

"It must be in there," says the handler.

"I can see it! Okay, I'll get it out." The Chief Conductor leaps into action and moves toward the gate of the stallion yard.

"I wouldn't do that if I were you, Chief Conductor. His name is Barracuda for a reason."

The Chief Inspector is going to ignore me and starts lifting the chain of the gate but jumps back quickly as the stallion charges at him, mouth wide open, with bared teeth and ears flattened back.

"Woah, boy, woah, I'm not going to hurt you. I just want to come in and get that phone in there."

The stallion glares at him silently until the Chief Conductor steps back.

"What are we going to do now?" asks the dog handler. "Maybe the dog and I can distract him, and you dash in through the rails and get it."

This idea is abandoned quickly as Barracuda keeps his eyes on both the dog and the Chief Inspector. He charges at the human but not the dog. Mr. Brown is lucky to save his man bun from Barracuda's teeth.

"I have a better idea. Why don't you take your magic wand there, Miss Clay, the thing you call a twitch, and subdue this beast so I can get the phone? I can see it clearly now."

"Me? You want me to go in there to get the phone for you? And get my head ripped off by the stallion? Are you insane?"

"Didn't you tell me this gadget is used to calm a horse and subdue it so it can be handled?"

"That's true, but that goes only for tame horses and this one isn't tame with me. He's only tame with Leonard, I think. Why don't you wait until he's back?"

By this time everyone has joined the audience around the yard.

"No, by the time he's back, the horse will have destroyed the phone, and we can't let that happen. You will have to use your vet skills to get it for us or tranquilize it so we can get it."

"First of all, all of you stand back, please, and especially that dog. Let me think about what I can do," I say. Thankfully, everyone, including the police officers, moves toward the hayshed. Precious looks up at me once they're gone.

"He's safe for you. I'll help," she says. Her voice sounds a little like Nan but with a slight European accent that I can't place.

"Precious, thank you. Is he really safe?" She blinks at me once.

I take the twitch off my belt and slowly approach the fence rails. The stallion stands right next to the phone, his right front foot squashing the loop of the leather phone cover into the sand.

"Don't twitch him; just touch him with it; he'll follow your orders," says Precious.

In slow motion, one leg goes over the lowest rail, my right hand with the twitch pointing in the stallion's direction. Once I am through, I straighten up, and before I move toward him, I decide to apologize to him for the hassle we put him through.

"Hi, Lightning, I know that's your name even though they call you Barracuda. Sorry to interrupt your siesta, but we need this phone under your right front leg. I'll leave immediately after picking your foot up unless you want to step off it by yourself."

The stallion does not move; his eyes are fixed on my face.

"He understands what you are saying," says Precious, who has followed me into the yard. "Don't be fearful. He is Olga's horse."

"I understand, Precious; he is Olga's familiar."

"Olga is Leonard's wife. The lady with the cello. She would want to know why Michael was killed."

I nod, a little nervous and jittery.

"Lightning, I am coming over now." I walk as fearlessly as I can muster toward the stallion, the twitch held out in front of me as if it were a peace offering. He is not moving. As I stand next to him, I realize he is the tallest and most perfect piece of horse flesh I have ever seen.

"Please step aside for a moment." I gently touch his right shoulder with the twitch, and he lifts his foot to step off the phone case.

"Thank you, Lightning. I very much appreciate what you are doing. I'll let you know what we find out."

I bend down slowly, pick up the phone, and look into the stallion's eyes as he lowers his head to my hand. The eyes are deep lakes of black volcanic glass, filled with wisdom but not evil. I stretch my left hand to his nose for him to take in my scent.

"Thank you," I say again and turn to walk out. I don't look back and hand the phone to the Chief Inspector.

"Thank you, Miss Clay. Very much appreciated." His voice has lost the tinge of arrogance and has taken on a more respectful tone.

"Pays to have a magic twitch. Can I go now?" I pet Precious, who has silently followed me out of the stallion yard.

"Sure, we'll analyze the phone and see what's on it. In the meantime, we won't bother you anymore. By the way, have you heard from Rocky, your neighbor, recently?"

"Yes, as a matter of fact, he sold me some hay yesterday."

"I think I'm going to see him on our way back. That saves me another trip out here. Goodbye, Miss Clay."

"Thank you for speaking today. I am so glad you did because I wouldn't have dared to go in with the stallion without you telling me it was safe."

Chapter 35

I feel elated to have been able to touch the stallion. What a magnificent horse. On my way to the trainers, I wonder who Olga really is. Another question for Ghostie tonight.

Alan is already waiting for me; his helpers and horses all lined up in their stable.

"Sorry for being late; the Chief Inspector paid us another visit. We couldn't just fob him off."

"What did he want? He obviously hasn't solved the case yet, and I doubt he ever will," says Alan.

"Why? They found Michael's phone and took it away for analyzing his texts and pictures."

"He won't have much on it. Mostly Raptor pictures and girls, I presume. Where did they find the phone? Wasn't it lost?"

"Yes, it had disappeared, but it turned up again in the stallion yard. Very strange."

"How did it get there? The stallion wouldn't have let anyone into the yard."

"Someone could have thrown it in there, or it could have been there all the time," I suggest.

"Well, it has nothing to do with us, so it doesn't concern us. Can you please give the blood samples to Nerida?

"I will, no worries." I pack up the rack of test tubes and drive back, letting the radio blare out the open car window. George would love to keep me company. I feel so guilty for keeping him locked up. I'll ask Rocky if he wants to borrow him for some work when he picks me up later for our drive to the cemetery.

Back at the hospital I find Nerida busy with the Mass Spectrometer.

"Hi Nerida, here are the samples from today. They want the results tonight, Alan said. It's about the horses for the picnic races on the weekend."

"Put them on the bench. I'll do them when I am finished here. Hehehe."

Lei walks in.

"Very strange that the phone just turned up today," he says.

"How did it get there?" asks Nerida.

"Yes, how indeed? And why there and why now? And where was it before it turned up in the stallion yard, I wonder," as if I had uncovered a secret but was unwilling to share my thoughts."

"And more importantly, who put it there and why?" mumbles Lei.

"I think it was always there, and the stallion just switched it on now," suggests Nerida.

"No way. Stallions can't switch on phones. Their feet are not made for it. They would be able to switch them off by crushing them, but not switching on," says Lei.

How do I get them both to tell me whether they know there is a maze? I need to give them a little hint.

"The phone was covered in soil that looked like the soil in the garden beds here or near the hedge."

"Maybe someone threw it in there," says Nerida. Lei shakes his head.

"But where was it the whole time until now? They only found it from its pings, so it must have been somewhere else until then. Someone wanted it found, I think."

"Great idea, Lei," I say. "But who would that someone be?"

I wait for Nerida's answer, but she seems unwilling to share her thoughts. If she were the killer, she would have taken the phone, deleted all the messages if she could, and buried it in the rabbit warren. Maybe Michael's phone had some kind of security so it couldn't be opened.

She must be terrified by the fact that it turned up and she doesn't know who found the phone.

"I wonder how the killer got here in the first place?" I continue. "I think he came past my cottage because my dog barked that night. Or they came from the mansion."

Nerida smiles as if I made a brilliant suggestion.

"They could have come from the farm down the road. He would have come past your cottage. The police are interviewing him now. So, it must be him. We have all been cleared so far. Hehehe"

"But it would have to have been someone who knew their way around the mansion and came through there. There must be holes in the hedge to crawl through if you want. Or they came along the driveway to the mansion and the manufacturing shed from the highway. Is there anyone else living in the mansion who could be a suspect?"

"Only Leonard and his wife. But they never mentioned any holes in the hedge," says Nerida.

"Why would they, Nerida? They don't need to crawl through holes. They use their gate to get from the mansion. But you know your way around the mansion gardens, don't you? You visited Michael in his flat. Maybe you went through the hedge."

"I don't crawl through holes in mazes. I leave that to others. Hehehe."

"I didn't say anything about mazes. Just hedges. Is there a maze?"

"Everyone knows about the maze, hehehe."

"I didn't know about a maze," says Lei.

"But there must be a reason Michael got killed that had nothing to do with mazes. What was it? I think it must have something to do with either a relationship or some shady horse business. According to the Chief Inspector, someone killed him around midnight and not at 4am when his phone texted me. That was only to confuse everyone into thinking he was still alive, giving the killer an alibi. Where did the phone go after 4am, and where did the sender go?"

I stare at Nerida, who is facing me with an arrogant expression.

"It was probably the farmer," she says, confident that that is the end of the conversation.

"Couldn't be," I say. "He has no idea how to handle an anesthetic machine or choose the right tranquilizers to incapacitate a big, burly man like Michael. I think your theory is faulty, Nerida."

"She could be right, though," interjects Lei. "He deals with cattle, and they are a lot heavier than Michael."

"You are living in Gaga Land. Riona," says Nerida, covering the Mass Spectrometer with its plastic hood. "Your twitchery out there with the stallion has gone to your head." She grabs the test tube rack to feed them into the blood analyzer.

Lei raises his eyebrows and winks at me to follow him outside.

"Why did you need to stir her up that much? If she is the killer, she knows that you suspect her, and you are in danger. Be careful."

"I will. Thanks for the warning, Lei."

I open the door to the lab again to stir up Nerida a little more.

"Nerida, I'm out this evening. Farmer Rocky is picking me up after work to take me for a sightseeing tour of the district. Not sure when I'll be back home. If you need me to assist in surgery, just call me. I'll call your phone, so you have my number, just in case."

She waves me off without a word.

Chapter 36

I spend the rest of the morning at the cottage, exploring the round garden bed in front, just in case Leonard extends my contract. Maybe I can grow some flowers and herbs. The thing is totally overgrown with weeds and grass, a few old lavender bushes, and ancient rose bushes that need urgent help to survive another season. George uses his freedom to gallop after magpies on the ground who fly off just out of his reach to tease him. A willy wagtail harasses the back of his head, and he tries to snap at it in futility.

Princess wanders over to me and lets me stroke her neck and forehead. Her coat glistens in the sun and has a rusty sheen to it that makes her look like a silver-gilded sculpture. She walks off to her hay bale, seemingly content in her new home. Then I remember she was Nan's horse, and this was her home in the past.

Where is Precious? I can't see her and don't find her inside, either. I may as well give Nan a call to update her and ask her a few questions about Olga and the cemetery before I visit it with Rocky.

She answers straightaway.

"Good morning, gorgeous."

"Nan, it's way past lunchtime. You must have been sleeping in. Or are you trying to prank me?"

"I wouldn't do such a thing, Riona. A little tricolored cat told me all about your taming of the black beast. Only he isn't a beast after all."

Her silvery bell laughter rings in my ear.

"Nan, what's the story with him? He obviously can understand what I say. Is he someone's familiar?"

"He's Olga's familiar."

"Who is this Olga? Is she Leonard's wife, the one who plays the cello? But why is she not interacting with us?"

"Yes, the one who plays the cello."

"Her name sounds Russian?"

"She is Russian and doesn't speak much English. Leonard met her in London, and they got married there. I am a little dubious about her. As she has such a powerful familiar, I think she is a powerful witch. I haven't heard anything about her creating any chaos or evil events while she's been here, though."

"Doesn't it say in your book of spells that witches have to be kind and use their powers only for good? Maybe she's a good witch. Why isn't she out and about on the property?"

"I don't know, Riona. Obviously, Precious and the stallion communicate. Maybe you could ask her about it."

"Nan, you were right about Precious. She finally spoke to me about how to address the stallion. She has a strange accent, too. Is she also from Russia?"

"I am glad she is talking to you. This means you are making progress as a witch, and she sees potential in you. As for her accent, she is from a long lineage of familiars. She could have originated from thereabouts. I mean Eastern Europe."

"Nan, I'm going to the cemetery with Rocky today. Is there anything I need to know before I go there?"

After a pause Nan gives me an evasive answer. "You will be fine; there is nothing spooky about it. You will find it interesting and informative."

"But will you be at the cemetery too?"

"It depends on what else is going on. I don't like cemeteries much. They are usually quite drab and heavy on the mind and soul. I'm more for lighthearted environs."

"And what about the bullet hole, Nan?"

She laughs too loudly and hangs up as if she hadn't heard my last question.

Chapter 37

During the afternoon, I help Lei with a lameness case that appeared out of the blue. Lei is very thorough, and his explanations for the owner are delivered in simple words without the scientific jargon that Nerida uses to impress clients. My respect for him grows.

A few minutes before 5 o'clock, I make a point of telling Nerida again that I am off on my tour of the district with Rocky and I might be back late as we may have dinner in town. She waves me off again, keeping her eyes focused on the screen of her computer.

On my way home, I wonder whether these short daily walks home and back to the hospital are enough to keep me fit. My rehab physio called today to find out how I am progressing and whether I'm keeping up my exercises and fitness work. I must admit that I greatly exaggerated my efforts over the last week.

I give George a run and quickly change into a new set of denim shorts with crystal sparkles and a white top with short sleeves. I am still not comfortable showing my scars, especially not to someone who might have an interest in me. His reaction will tell me whether he'll be put off by my imperfections and scarred legs. My brown Blundstone boots don't really match the sparkles of the shorts, but as I don't know whether I need to walk through long grass, they are a safe choice. To top it all off with flair, I tame my hair into a French Roll.

It doesn't take long before the 'meep meep' of the Nissan sounds at the front door. I lock George up before bolting out the front door.

"Wow, hold your horses," Rocky laughs. "We are going to a cemetery. Maybe a more somber speed is required."

I slow down to a snail's pace with mock regret.

"Just kidding. Hop in."

I can't get enough of his gray eyes. They radiate seriousness but also intense focus on whatever they look at.

Everything that usually sits in front of the passenger seat and well of his farm truck have been moved to make space for me.

He revs up the Nissan, and we turn out onto the Green Bowlder Road. After about two kilometers, he turns right again into a farm driveway.

"That is our place," he says. "I'll show you later."

We pass a couple of grain silos, a multi-blade windmill, a diesel bowser, and a large shearing shed on the left, and then a set of steel cattle pens. The house is separated from the farm yard by a row of large cypress trees. Rocky doesn't notice my curiosity about his farm.

"This is the only way to the cemetery now, other than from Leonard's place," he says, passing the house. "But I don't think anyone knows the cemetery exists, so nobody comes here to visit it. We only have another hour until sunset. It's actually quite peaceful just before dark."

The geography starts making sense to me now. After a couple more farm gates that Rocky asks me to open and shut behind us, I can see a patch of cypress and pine trees at the side of a slight hill. It is more of a gentle rise than a true hill. It has an old post and picket fence around it that's in need of a fresh coat of paint.

We step out into a grassy spot that's hard underfoot but surrounded by thigh-high graying grass.

"I don't come here often. I leave it undisturbed, so I cut the grass only on the outside perimeter to keep the fire hazard as low as possible. Let's see if I can find the lady from the picture."

I follow hesitantly at first, aware of the possibility of a snake feeling disturbed by our presence, but Rocky doesn't seem to worry.

"Ah, here she is."

Rocky points at the granite statue in front of us as we pass the trunk of a spreading cypress. The statue is smaller than I had imagined, only about half a meter high and on a square pedestal. Overall, it's just high enough for her stone eyes to gaze across the grasses surrounding her.

I approach her hesitantly, as if I'm intruding on her space, and walk once around her. The pedestal is tilted slightly, sunken into the earth at its east corner.

Rocky watches me silently, a grass stalk between his teeth.

"She does look like the lady in the picture," he says softly.

"Let me see who she is," I say, pretending I have no clue.

I kneel down in front of the pedestal and read the inscription, faded and weathered by years of harsh Australian climate.

Elena Wilhemine Anderson
Born 12 August 1900
Died 25 November 1956

A hot, stabbing pain rushes from my chest to my throat. This is the same woman. It's Nan's mother, Elena.

My mind races. Elena must have died here. She wasn't very old, just fifty-six. How did she die? Her daughter, my Nan, would have been just fourteen years old then. Why did she never talk about her? Why did Mum never mention that she died so young?

I stand up, my eyes still fixed on the grave, trying to keep a calm face.

"Let's see who else is here."

Rocky leads me around the trees until we find another grave. This time, the grave of an old man with a foreign name, born in Afghanistan, who died on the Anderson Estate.

"There used to be Afghan people here who came from South Australia, where they had been camel train drivers. Maybe he came here to work in the Gold Fields," says Rocky.

Then, we find another grave that is overgrown with an ancient rose bush. A few scented apricot-colored blooms look fragile but are a sign of an optimistic future ahead, of persistence, survival, and eternal beauty. Precious sits under the rose bush, the orange of her fur glowing in the fading sunlight.

"What are you doing here, Precious?" I ask, but she pretends she doesn't see me.

"Look, there's another grave here with a plaque," says Rocky.

I move the grass away to expose the white enamel plaque and the slab of stone under it.

Friederike Wilhelmine Woynewitsch
Born 31 May 1874
Died 25 November 1956

My mind spins. Nan's grandmother. Elena's mother. She did come with her daughter Elena to Australia. Elena Anderson, who took over her English husband's landholdings. Why did my family keep silent about this? And why did they move away from here?

Why did she die on the same day as Elena? And how did they die? Does the bullet hole in the door have anything to do with it?

I suddenly feel a deep sorrow rising in my chest. As the sun tinges the grasses around me, the rose petals turn a blood orange. Rocky stands beside me and puts his hand on my shoulder ever so lightly. My eyes finally let the tears fall.

"Oh no, I didn't think it would affect you so much."

I try to compose myself, blinking away my tears. "Are there any other graves here?"

"I don't know. I might come out here with the whippersnapper and clear the grass. We would probably find more."

I nod silently and turn toward the Nissan. Precious has disappeared. Why did she come here?

"It looks like this Friederike was Elena's mother," says Rocky. "They must have bought the Anderson Estate at some stage. I wonder whether it was divided and sold after they both died."

My tears start flowing again, but I'm also furious, angry at my mother, who kept this whole family history from me. Why? But I don't tell him that I already know that Elena and Friederike are daughter and mother.

"I want to check out the Anderson Estate history a bit more."

"I know a couple of people who can help you with that. There is an old schoolteacher who taught in the fifties and sixties, and there would be the property records at the shire office. Maybe after the whole murder affair is over, we can have a look into it. What do you think?"

Rocky holds the door of the Nissan open for me. I'm sure he doesn't want me to hang around here getting more miserable.

"I'll introduce you to my granddad if you like," he suggests.

"Sure." I'm actually not sure if that is a good idea, but it would be rude to say no and go back home just to read the Paranormal Monthly article again for anything I might have missed. And Ghostie can wait for a chat, too. I am really cross with her for keeping her family secrets from me. Considering she wants me to be a proper witch and learn more witchcraft skills, but told me nothing about the witches who taught her these skills. Bad Nan.

Chapter 38

Rocky parks the Nissan at his house and walks ahead of me to his back door, where there is a pile of men's boots. They give the impression that the house is devoid of women.

He opens the door to a dark corridor and calls inside.

"Hi Pop, are you in? I brought our new neighbor along to meet you."

From deep inside the house comes a grunt that only Rocky can interpret. He smiles at me, and his gray eyes sparkle mischievously, making my heart flutter in my chest.

"Come on in."

I follow him to the living room, where an old man watches TV from a recliner chair. He gets up as we enter. He is a giant of a man, tall but not fat or spongy. He is an older version of Rocky, only about a foot taller.

"Pop, this is Riona. She's a new vet from up the road. She lives in the old Anderson Cottage."

Pop nods and shakes my hand, while intensely studying my face, then looks at Rocky, clenching his jaws. "I see. One of them," he says and sits down again.

I look curiously at the old man, wondering what he meant.

"We were up at the cemetery, Pop, and I'm wondering if we shouldn't have a bite to eat before I drop her home a little later."

"You might want to pick something from the freezer and defrost it in the microwave. I haven't done any cooking yet."

I follow Rocky into the kitchen, and he hands me a can of Coke from the fridge.

"I hope you don't mind Coke. I haven't had time to go shopping this week. We're just pregnancy-testing the cows to off-load the ones that didn't take. But we'll be finished with that on Friday."

"Who is doing the testing?"

"Ah, the vets from up the other way, your competition. We can't afford your prices." He laughs, but not in a way that is meant to embarrass me.

I take the Coke into the living room while Rocky puts a container of butter chicken into the microwave to defrost and sets up a couple of cups of rice in their rice cooker.

"I hope this is okay with you? We have a lot of Indian food when we are busy."

He hands a can of beer to Pop, and we sit in the living room again.

Taking a sip of his beer, Pop's eyes scan my face wordlessly. He puts the beer down on the small octagonal table beside him and looks up at Rocky.

"She definitely is one of them. I can see the family resemblance," he says, nodding in my direction.

"What family resemblance?" asks Rocky.

"The Andersons. The Anderson girls."

I feel the blood rise to my head and am glad that it is almost dark in the room. The lightning bolt from before at Elena's grave is striking again in my chest.

"The Anderson girls?" I ask with a slightly croaky voice.

"Pop, what are you talking about?"

"She looks like the young girl who lived there. I think it was in the early fifties. At least until she moved away. She would have been about twelve or so. A teenager, I think. Do you think you have Anderson blood in you, young Lady?"

"I don't really know, I think I might have, but I am not sure whether it would be these Andersons."

"They were bad news, the bloody lot of them, ever since they set foot on this land."

"When did you meet them, and what were their names?" I ask, to brush over the awkwardness of being ignorant of my family tree.

"Aw, there was one called Ana, I think. She was the mother of the young girl. I think her name was something to do with a bird.

In my mind, I fill in the blanks. That must have been Robyn, my mother.

He is talking about Nan and my mom.

"When was that?" I ask.

"That was after they sold but before they moved away, in the sixties. I was a young lad then, but I didn't take much interest in them. It was better not to. The daughter was too young for me, and the mother too old. But it wasn't a pleasant time with all the dividing of the property and the vultures diving in to get ahold of a part of it. My dad was lucky enough to be able to buy our place. The Scotts bought the place where their grandson eventually built the vet clinic. And further up they cut off a chunk for a horse stud and training center. That place changed hands several times. All in all, not a happy place, the Anderson's Estate. But luckily, they couldn't sell the Green Bowlder and so it was turned into a State Forest for all to use."

I keep silent, determined to have a serious talk with Nan before I divulge that this Ana was my Nan and Elena, her mother. Why on earth was I destined to come to this place, back to where they came from?

I make conversation with Pop, asking about his sheep and cows and Rocky about his dogs. His gray eyes try to lock on to mine to break through the barriers I've erected to protect myself from more Anderson Estate secrets.

After dinner, Rocky and I wash the dishes while he talks about his dogs and the fire brigade. He says it's his passion, trying to figure out how to manage the land and keep the fire risk down in summer. He gives talks at schools, hoping to encourage young people to become volunteers.

I decide I like Rocky; his easygoing charm, the awkward movements around the house, the confident strides in the paddock, and the company of his dogs and Princess.

"Rocky, do you need another dog for work? My dog is so bored in his kennel all day. I don't mind if you take him for some work. I'm not sure how good a muster dog he is, but Dad used him for his sheep and was happy with him. He gave him to me as a watchdog and for protection."

"Let's wait until they've solved the murder. It might be better if he lives with you until then. I might try him out one day when you have a day off, and you can watch his work. We can make a decision then, if that's okay with you."

"Super. I hope this case will be solved soon. It's getting on my nerves; I don't like unsolved problems. Wow, it's almost eleven. I think it's time to get home, Rocky. Thank you so much for the dinner."

I shake hands with Pop again. "I'll talk to my mother about how we would fit into this Anderson story, if we fit at all. I'll let you know and maybe ask you more questions later."

He lifts his hands as if to salute but stays seated in his recliner.

"Pop is full of arthritis. Cattlework takes it out of you. Dad is working on the oil rigs in Western Australia and can't help. But he earns good money, so we can afford to keep farming."

Rocky chats away the few minutes until he rounds the garden of my cottage to shine his headlights on the front door.

"Do you want to come in for a cup of tea or coffee before you drive home?"

"No thanks, I better not. I need to get up early tomorrow to muster for Dad, so the vets can get going straightaway."

He waves his hand as if trying to reach the brim of his hat, which he isn't wearing now.

I open the door of the Nissan and stumble, misjudging the distance to the ground.

Princess neighs at the gate, once, twice, three times. What bee has gotten under her bonnet?

"Are you okay? I'll wait until you are inside so you don't trip in the dark."

I wave goodbye to his gray eyes that sparkle in the interior light, slightly annoyed about my clumsy exit.

"She's worried that I might trip, the good soul," I say as if that was a good explanation for Princess neighing. "Good night, Rocky. Happy mustering tomorrow."

I run up to the front door, trying to appear light-footed in my Blundstones. Without a stumble, I wave to him. He puts his car into gear and drives off onto the road.

Chapter 39

I t takes a few seconds to adjust my eyes to the darkness. The moon, slightly thinner today, has risen high
over our small home and gives Princess in her paddock
a ghostly silver sheen. She stopped neighing but still
stands at the gate, waiting for me.

"What's up, Princess? Don't worry, I'm back. I was out
with Rocky," I say as I walk up to her gate. Her white coat
is streaked with sweat.

"What's wrong, Princess? Are you sick? Wait here, I'll
just get the thermometer to take your temperature." I
shine my phone torch onto her gums. "They look fine.
Don't worry. We'll get this sorted in a minute, as soon as
I switch the porch light on."

I run to the cottage and open the door to reach the
light switch in the living room.

When I come to, I'm disoriented; on the hallway floor,
tangled in the coat stand that somehow tripped me up
when I speeded through the door.

"What the ... ?"

Unfolding my legs from under the sturdy piece of furniture, feeling for my phone, but can't find it. What the heck happened here?

Moving to the front door, I switch on the hallway light.

A slight draft coming from the kitchen tells me that I must have left the back door open in my excitement to meet Rocky for our cemetery adventure. The click of the light switch, however, reveals a picture of chaos.

The kitchen chairs are in the hallway. The hair on the back of my neck rises in fear. I shake in my boots and laugh nervously at the cliché, but I do actually shake in terror of who might still lurk in the house.

"Hello, anybody here?" I call out. No answer.

Who did this? I hold my breath and listen into the darkness of the house.

"Precious? George?" I whisper, hoping for a sound from either of them.

No answer. Precious is probably talking to Lightning, catching mice or something better for dinner. I creep forward and wish I had my Twitch with me. It would be a small tool for defending myself, but better than nothing.

I trip over a pile of books on the floor in the living room and switch on the light.

"Oh my ... !" The room is chaos; everything turned upside down and ripped apart. The beautiful sofa has its cushions ripped off the frame, and the grid of the fireplace has been torn out to reveal what might be up in the chimney. What I had placed on the bookshelves is now on the floor; the books have been leafed through.

I race to the kitchen, switching on any light I can find, and out the back door. George stands at the door, tail between his legs, frightened and giving me tiny whiny sounds. I let him out, and he presses his body against my legs, still scared and hoping I can give him strength.

He follows me inside, keeping body contact.

"Where is my phone, George?"

I find it where I dropped it when I tripped over the coat stand. My magic twitch has rolled under the fridge, but having found it makes me feel safer. Confident that Princess' sweating is the result of her panic due to the noise of breaking furniture, I take a towel from my bedroom to dry her sweat and console her.

I give her a cup of pellets to distract her and go back inside to assess the full extent of the damage. I am confident that whoever was responsible for it has left.

Elena's portrait had been ripped off the wall, and the paper at its back sliced open.

Ditto the other painting in the spare bedroom. I hang both of them back on their hooks, apologizing for the inconvenience of having been ripped off so unceremoniously.

Then I realize that the vandals have not found the little door in the corner of the living room. The paneling is untouched and the green upholstered chair that had been next to the fireplace is now turned upside down on top of the green trunk in front of the door, protecting it from being opened accidentally.

"Now, what do I do?" I say to George, who is still clinging to me. I turn the chair right side up, pushing it back to its original place to sit down. George hops on my lap, pressing against my chest with my arms wrapped around him for comfort, as I stare at the mess in front of me.

"You should call your Chief Inspector, I think, or Rocky," whispers Nan near my head.

"Oh, Nan, this is so devilish. Who did this, and why did they have to destroy my home? Why, Nan?"

"You know who, and you know why." Nan's voice sounds confident, and my pulse slows down.

"Is it because of the Andersons in the cemetery?" I am still absorbed in the revelation of the past few hours.

"Don't be ridiculous, Riona. No, no, no, not at all. It's much closer to here."

"What is the story of them and this cottage? There must be a connection."

"Listen, darling, you are confused. You knocked your head when you came in and passed out. Wake up! It has nothing to do with them, we'll talk about them later. Some time later. Think about the here and now."

Refocusing, I stroke George again and again. Of course, she's right. It has to do with Michael's murder. It must have been Nerida. I told her I was going to be out until late, and she's still looking for her blood result sheets. Of course. That's it.

"You got it, kid," whispers Nan. I can see her fist-pumping in my mind, as she always did when I mastered a new skill with my pony when I was little.

"Call the Chief Conductor now. Tell him what you think about these papers."

"I don't know why she wants them. There is no point in telling him about them if I can't tell him why they are important."

"They must have something to do with the horse races. Maybe they are switching horses. At least, that is what they did in my days. Pump up a horse for a few races until it is the favorite, then switch it with a dud that looks like it, and the punters lose on the races. Or they have a dud run a few poor races and then switch him for a good one."

"Nan, that time is well and truly gone. They're all microchipped now, and you can't do that anymore. It must have something to do with her research and with the trainers, but I don't know what."

"Why don't you let the Chief Inspector work that out, hmm? These people are far too dangerous to solve this riddle by yourself. They might get to you before you have worked it out. Like they got to your house first."

I get up from the chair and clip the twitch to my belt. I find the clinic phone that the Chief Inspector gave back to me in the bedroom and stick it into my left back pocket and Nan's phone into my right one.

"I have a much better idea, Nan. Leave it to me."

Chapter 40

Nerida is on duty, and I hope she isn't out on a call. There's only one way of finding out what's going on, and that is to confront her. I leave Nan on her chair next to the fireplace, hoping she will stay there and not come hurtling after me to the hospital.

George follows me closely to ensure I don't leave him behind.

"It's ok, George, you will be my protector," I smile at him and pat his head. He huffs in anticipation of mustering sheep in the dark.

"Come on, George, let's walk."

"Are you sure you want to do this?" asks a small voice at my feet. The accent tells me that Precious has returned.

"Yes, I am. I am going to do this."

Precious gives a sigh that sounds too big for her small body.

"I'll carry you, so you don't have to walk. You must be exhausted after the walk to and from the cemetery."

I bend down and lift up Precious onto my shoulder. She is surprisingly light.

"You need to hold on by yourself," I say as we get on our way, the moon still high and letting us see any obstacles on the ground. Didn't I say I needed exercise and that walking was a good idea? How many times did I walk this brick path this week?

I'm sure Nerida isn't expecting me to turn up in the middle of the night. I hope she's a night owl and still in the staff room watching TV or reading her textbooks. I wonder if she expects the police to turn up after the cottage break-in.

I sneak around the hospital building to make sure nobody else has arrived in the parking area. I don't worry about the motion sensors that have lit up like daylight, showing me that the hay shed is now full of hay bales. At least a sign that busier days are expected.

The stallion comes over to the rails and softly nickers at us.

"Hey, Lightning. Please don't turn out a racket. We're going to be busy, but Precious and George are coming with me to help."

He sticks his head out through the rails and nuzzles Precious, who rubs her head against his nose.

"So, you are friends. Fancy that," I say, glad to see that the stallion has accepted me as a friend rather than an enemy of the infamous 'Barracuda', the horror horse of the district.

"Let's go, kids," I say to George and Precious as I move toward the hospital breezeway. Precious obviously doesn't like to be called a kid and digs her claws into my neck.

"Sorry, Precious, I just meant George."

I know George isn't the bravest dog, and I've never been in a situation where I had to test his loyalty or courage, but today might be his day.

The roller door is open a foot wide, and I squeeze through, hoping that Precious manages to hang on to me.

I hear the TV upstairs in the staff room. Phew; that means Nerida is still up. She must be disappointed, having left my cottage empty-handed.

I don't want to confront her in the staff room. It's too small to allow me to get out of her way in case she lunges at me. Better to talk to her down in the breezeway with the heavy horse crush between me and her.

"Nerida?" I call up to the staff room. "Nerida?"

The sound of her blocky heels clunks down the stairs. When she appears in the dark breezeway, I immediately know I should have switched the light on before she came down, but she does me the favor and does it herself.

"What took you so long?" she says with an air of superiority and turns toward the Laboratory.

Always the pompous fountain of all knowledge, she needs to demonstrate she was expecting me.

Precious, on my neck, puffs up into a fur ball twice her normal size and claws my skin, expecting I might leap to the side. She's obviously scared. Can she read Nerida's mind?

Nerida holds the door open for me. Conscious that she's about twenty kilos heavier than me and much stronger, I worry my only recently stitched-together body might not be up to a fight with her if it came to that. I need to be careful.

"After you," I say. She lets the door go. I stop it from body-slamming me and step inside the Lab. A few steps ahead of me, Nerida moves toward the long bench with the blood machines, the microscopes, and the mass spectrometer. Her eyes roam along the bench as if searching for something, but I can't see what that might be.

Nerida turns and, leaning her back on the bench, spreads out her arms on either side, exuding an air of confidence that signals she is in total control over the situation.

"What did you mean 'took me so long' Nerida?"

She fixes her eyes on me, not uttering another word for a few seconds, then sighs as if explaining the most basic facts of life to a five-year-old.

"So, you've finally figured it out, haven't you? Hehehe-he." Her nervous laugh is even more annoying without any other audience.

I realize she's not as confident as she wants me to believe.

I pretend to put my hands into the back pockets of my shorts and wish I had changed into another, more comfortable pair. Both mobile phones are hidden from Nerida. How can I switch my phone on without her noticing it so it can record what she says? The only way is to sit down on a lab stool at the table in the middle of the lab to hide my hands.

"Why don't you tell me what I supposedly have found out?" I say calmly, pulling my phone from its back pocket and switching it on. It's a little difficult to find the recording app without her noticing, but I manage. Phew!

Nerida answers with a high-pitched scream of a laugh, as if my question was a great joke.

I need to make her talk and confess to whatever scheme she's part of. Maybe she killed Michael.

"Are you admitting, then, that you turned my cottage upside down to find your papers?"

She sighs as if I am daft.

"Of course, I did that. That wasn't hard for you to work out."

"But you didn't find them?"

"No, I didn't, but that doesn't matter anymore anyway."

"Why is that?" I'm short of ideas for how to get her to tell me why she was after those blood results.

"Because you have only one option now. I am giving you the same choice that I gave Michael, and if you're smart, you'll take it."

"And what if I'm not?"

"That would be surprising for someone with an Honors degree. You would make the same mistake that Michael made. I thought he was smarter, but obviously, he wasn't the sharpest tool in the toolbox. Too focused on his womanizing."

"It was you who killed him. Because he left you for someone else?"

"Have I said that? He just didn't take me up on my offer. He could have saved himself."

"What is this special offer that wasn't good enough for Michael?"

"I offered him part of the profit, but he wanted more. He wasn't satisfied with what he got. He wanted more and more without making it worthwhile for me."

"So, one day, you said enough is enough?"

"Exactly."

Nerida moves along the bench toward the door again. I move in the direction opposite to where she wants me to go. She seems to change her mind, moving back to her previous position at the bench.

"What was the proposition you made him?" I ask, pretending I might be interested in her offer.

"That doesn't matter anymore now. It's far too late for that, don't you think, hehehehe?"

"Why is that?" I say as calmly as I can manage, placing my phone on the lab stool next to me and pushing it further under the table. I hope it will record properly from there.

Precious decides to jump off my shoulder and onto the bench. She walks toward Nerida as if she wants a head scratch, tail held high, and purr motor in top gear. George is walking around the table, sniffing at the furniture and the rubbish bin. I wish I had left him at home because he isn't a great indoor helper. I'm no match for Nerida.

Nerida looks down at Precious, momentarily distracted. I take the opportunity and dash to the door but trip over George. He anticipated my movement and leaped toward the door before me.

I crash to the floor, Nan's phone cluttering out of my shorts pocket and sliding toward Nerida, who dives on me with her full weight. As I reach for the phone, she slams her boot down on my wrist and reaches to turn the door lock.

"Hahaha! Now, what do you do?"

Yes, what do I do now? This is the third time today I have tripped, literally. My French Roll has unraveled, and my hair hangs around my face like a tattered curtain, obscuring my view.

Nerida bends down and picks up Nan's phone. I hope she doesn't see the other one on the lab chair, but she's too focused on me.

What are my options? Precious is still sitting on the bench, watching as Nerida places the phone beside her. I stand up and face them both, pretending to be a little disoriented but secretly hoping Precious has some witchcraft trick up her paws to get us out of this predicament.

"It doesn't pay to be disabled if you are a vet," Nerida says. "You are far too clumsy and slow for this profession. Your little twitch is not going to save you from being a failed vet. I will put you out of your misery, yes? heheheheh." As if that is a great joke.

"And how are you going to do that, Nerida? Same way as Michael?"

"Yes, exactly, but don't worry, it won't hurt. Sit down, Riona; it will make it easier for you and for me."

I look at Precious, and she blinks at me twice.

Does this mean I should do what Nerida says? Precious blinks again.

I sit down again opposite Nerida, who now reaches behind one of the microscopes and pulls out a syringe. The syringe isn't large, but I can see that it contains a clear liquid.

"So you knew I would come, and you prepared for me?"

She holds the syringe up in front of her face, giving it an admiring glance. A little smile crosses her eyes. She gives me a calculating look, pretending I might be interested in the scientifically optimal concentration of the tranquilizer mix she has mixed up for me.

"This is a very special cocktail I designed for you that I learned in South Africa when I worked with wildlife. It will make you drowsy, and after a couple of minutes, you won't be able to walk or stand up. You will still be able to talk for a little while, but not for long. And then you will go to sleep."

The thought of this all being recorded gives me some satisfaction, but I worry that she might find the phone on the lab chair under the table and destroy it. Better to stay alive, I reprimand myself.

She holds the syringe up and squeezes the trigger to push out any tiny air bubbles. Looking at it again and then at me, she is visibly working out how to inject me without a struggle.

My mouth is dry, and I start trembling from fear and anger at being so stupid and getting myself into this situation.

Nerida smiles as she sees my despair and leans back. Initially, I think she wants to torture me a little more, but then she lifts her arm. I try to judge which way she's going to throw and which way I should duck to ensure she misses her one and only shot.

As if in slow motion, I see her hand with the syringe rise up next to her head for the throw when Nan's phone neighs. It neighs with the ferociously loud scream of a horse in distress. The sound echoes around the hard surfaces of the lab and slices through Nerida's almost soothing voice.

The shocking sound startles her, causing the to drop the syringe. Unable to adjust the power behind the toss, the needle of the syringe penetrates the jeans of her right thigh. The syringe is stuck. It has made its mark, and the liquid drains out of it in slow motion, steadily but inevitably, until it is empty.

Nerida's eyes open wide in horror. The phone stops neighing, and silence resumes. Precious walks over to

Nerida and head-bumps her shoulder. Nerida slides off her lab chair and now sits on the floor, leaning against a cupboard door.

"And now, what do we do?"

Yes, what do I do? If I leave her here and go home, she will surely die. If I call triple zero, they will probably take half an hour to get here. They still might not be able to save her. And I'll be the suspect. Again. Nobody will believe that she tried to kill me, and a horse-neighing ringtone shocked Nerida into injecting herself instead of me. They won't believe me. What can I do?

"How much time have you got, Nerida?" She probably thinks I'm googling tranquilizers and antidotes.

"Maybe fifteen minutes, tops. You must help me, Riona. I'll make you a partner and give you 80% of the profit. You won't need to work anymore, I promise. You need to give me the antidote. I'll tell you what to use. I will completely recover if you give me the antidote. Nobody will ever need to know what happened here."

I stare at Precious for help, and she blinks again.

"Fifteen minutes? That is quite a while. So, just let me be clear, you will make me rich if I let you live? How can I trust you to keep your promise?

"I promise," she says, her voice filled with panic, no silly laughs this time.

"Tell me where the antidote is, how much I need to draw up, and how to get it into you. And then we talk."

The words tumble out of her mouth, and I rush to the pharmacy. The poison safe is locked.

"Nerida, where is the key?" I yell at her.

"Here!" She throws the key at me. Her throw isn't quite accurate, but I pick it up from the floor and open the safe. I pick up the glass vial with the antidote and go back to Nerida.

She is sweating a little now. Her breathing has slowed, too.

"Is this the right one?"

She nods, and I get a syringe from a tray. "How much?" She tells me. With the syringe filled, I sit down in front of her while pulling Nan's phone from her reach, and set it on voice recorder, too. Better two recordings than one. And she must not know that the other phone is recording already.

"Now, Nerida, just to make sure you keep your promise, you need to record what you promised and also tell me about the killing of Michael, the why and the how. The whole story, in summary, because you haven't much time left until your voice gives out. Be quick, because I won't give you the antidote until I have your story."

Nerida's voice slurs, and I hope she'll get her confession out before she passes out completely. I set Nan's phone in front of her on a chair and stand up, the antidote in my hand, and hear the story of a vet who has been bribed by the trainers to give their horses performance-enhancing drugs and use the mass spectrometer to work out how to optimize the doses for the best results. She had received part of the doped horses' prize money and also benefitted from bets made on her behalf.

Nerida has slumped down on her side. Her eyes are now fearful, and stare pleadingly at me. There will only be seven minutes left for the antidote to reverse the deadly cocktail she had designed herself.

I ram the antidote into her other thigh and hope she will keep talking before the antidote gives her the strength to stand up again.

"I need to get out, Nerida, just for a little while. I need some fresh air. I'll be back soon. It's not every day that I save someone's life. The stress makes me feel nauseous."

I turn Nan's phone off, leaving the other one to continue recording, and walk out into the breezeway.

Chapter 42

The cold chill of the night air in the breezeway makes me shiver as I call both the Chief Inspector and Rocky to come as fast as possible. I still don't trust that she won't overpower me and take the recording after the antidote has done its job.

Rocky says he'll be here in two minutes, and the Chief Inspector reminds me to keep the recording out of Nerida's hands and lock her in the lab until he arrives. The ambulance is on its way, and hopefully, they will take care of Nerida so she can be taken to prison, where she belongs.

When I get back into the lab, I see Nerida breathing more deeply again. Her fingers move, and then she lifts a shaking hand toward me.

"Thank you, Riona. I will keep my promise."

I don't contradict her belief that I'm going to be her new accomplice in race fixing from now on and sit on my lab chair again, waiting and hoping someone will come soon. My fear has made space for a feeling of emptiness and dread. Precious has hopped down from the bench and onto my lap. She bumps her head against my nose, purring. Does that mean I have lived up to her expectations?

Nerida's breathing sounds normal now, but she isn't trying to get up yet. The antidote is working as it should, but she doesn't seem to feel in a hurry to stand up. Maybe she's thinking about whether she can really trust me. Will I be greedy enough to become her partner in crime? There's still time enough for her to think about all the possibilities she imagines she has of spinning this drama in her favor. I won't disturb her thoughts.

But there are a few issues. How am I going to explain that Nan's phone rang and startled Nerida. I check its call register. Nothing. I'll just tell the Chief Conductor Nerida missed her throw. She will probably agree with me that a phone neighing isn't something to be proud of if you try to commit murder and miss your shot.

The stallion calls out in the yard and Princess answers. Maybe he told her I'm safe.

The screech of the roller door sounds like music to my ears. This must be Rocky.

"I'm here," I call out and tell George to bark. Nerida looks at me with an expression of arrogant disappointment and disgust, the corners of her mouth turned down, but she is still too weak to stand up.

"You witch! I knew it. Never trust a stupid witch like you."

"If only you knew!" I smile and wiggle my twitch at her. "I think I'd rather keep using my magic wand instead of doping horses and killing people."

I open the door of the lab for Rocky. He gives Nerida a brief look and seems to assess her as not dangerous. My disheveled appearance probably gives him the impression I'd been in a fight.

"What happened? What did she do?"

"She tried to kill me the same way she killed Michael."

"But didn't he get killed with your anesthetic machine?"

Nerida utters a weak laugh.

"No, he wasn't. I injected him with the tranquilizer when he had his back turned in the recovery box. I just had to lock him in there and wait until he dropped. When he was dead, I lifted him with the crane onto the operating table and put the breathing tube of the anesthetic machine in his mouth to confuse the situation. I wouldn't have done that to you, Riona. You would have been found in the pharmacy, stealing drugs. After all, you are probably a recovered addict after all the painkillers you had after your accident. Everyone would have believed that."

I am so glad I haven't stopped my phone recording under the table. Now I do have her complete confession.

"But why, Nerida? Why? You make good money here."

"Why not? More money is always better. And it was interesting. I worked out the perfect way of enhancing the performance of horses without being detected."

"Except I found your test sheets."

"Yes, unfortunately."

She tries to get up but is still too wobbly on her feet.

"Sit down, Nerida, it's no use. The Chief Inspector will be here in a minute, and Rocky will be able to deal with you until then."

Nerida sits down again, giving Rocky a glance.

"You two are like two peas in a pod, skinny as rakes, ugly, and devious as hell."

Rocky grins at me.

"Come on, little pea, sit down and call your boss. He might want to know that another one of his staff is leaving his employ. Maybe he'll offer you a full-time job now, considering the new vacancy."

"True, I might as well start by taking over the on-calls tonight."

"If the Chief Inspector lets you and doesn't tie you up in hours of interviews."

"He should be here by now," I say, looking at my watch. As if on cue, the wailing of an ambulance and police cruisers roars up the driveway. I meet them at the breezeway while Rocky monitors Nerida.

The Chief Inspector jumps out of his car as if stung by a hornet. His frizzy hair surrounds his head like a halo. He must have forgotten his hair tie. He reminds me of a wilted sunflower, slightly past his prime but still impressive.

"Hi, Chief Conductor," I greet him with a smile as if I had just experienced the most satisfying holiday adventure.

"I wish you wouldn't call me that, Miss Clay. Where is Nerida?"

"She's inside. Rocky is keeping an eye on her."

"So, you two have ganged up on her," he says as he rushes past me

"Nothing of the kind." I am getting anxious he might believe Nerida instead of me and Rocky. I had been his prime suspect, after all, just a few days ago.

He storms into the Lab and surveys the situation: Nerida on the floor, Rocky by the bench.

"I am so glad you are here now, Chief Inspector," says Nerida, her voice calm and convincing.

"What?" I say in disbelief. She has a nerve. Rocky rolls his eyes at the Chief Inspector.

"So where is this confession you recorded, Miss Clay?"

I hand him my phone from under the table. I hope it has recorded everything properly. "I didn't dare switch it off before you came or send the file to you, just in case I pressed the wrong button and deleted it by accident."

The Chief Inspector presses Play and listens to the recording. Nerida looks down on her hands.

"It was taken under duress," she says as if that was a logical answer.

"I am going to forward this file to the office now, but I will need to keep your phone for a little while to make sure you haven't recorded any other conversations that I might need."

"But I need it back, please, as soon as possible."

"Sure, but you still have your grandmother's phone. So, you are not out of reach and out of touch."

I put Nan's phone back in my pocket, glad that she can still reach me on it. I can't wait to tell her about tonight, but then I realize she probably already knows it and is hanging around here somewhere.

While the ambos are fussing over Nerida and the Chief Conductor is listening to the recording, Lei bursts into the Lab, followed by two uniformed police officers.

"What are you doing here, Lei?" I ask, trying to under-stand how he could know what was going on here.

"He's one of us, Miss Clay," says the Chief Inspector. He is from the Hong Kong police. As he happens to be also a horse vet, he was the perfect person to work undercover in this hospital to collect evidence about international horse race fixing and money laundering."

"Wow! So he's part of your little orchestra here, Chief Conductor," is the only thing that I am able to say.

"It's not a small orchestra, Miss Clay. On the contrary."

"Never mind, Riona," says Lei. "I had a good time here with you all."

The ambulance with Nerida in it is leaving, followed by one of the police cars. Uniformed police take stock of the poison safe and collect the evidence into evidence bags, the syringe that Nerida stabbed herself with, the blood analyzers and Mass spectrometer, and the discarded blood tubes from the sharps and biologicals bins.

I call Leonard and tell him that Nerida had an accident with a drug and is in hospital, as told by the Chief Inspector. He wants to make sure the training stable does not get any forewarning about the coming raid of their premises in the morning. He asks me to call Janice to take over the rest of the night shift and the next day.

The Chief Inspector ushers Rocky and me out of the lab and into reception and seals the lab door with police tape.

"Now, Miss Clay, thank you for your bravery, but I wonder how you knew that Nerida was involved in Michael's murder and the horse doping scheme."

"Both Michael and Nerida warned me to keep my nose out of things going on at the hospital. Michael's car was far too expensive for him to pay for it with just his salary from this job. So, it had to have something to do with horses and with money. Nerida's secretive behavior around the blood test results of the horses from up the road made me suspicious. And, she said, she deleted everything from the machines' memories, too. That's totally unnecessary. I found some of the test sheets in the bin and took them for safekeeping. When she couldn't find them, she got really frantic about them going missing."

"Unfortunately, we didn't find any sheets. So, there is no evidence of that."

"I have the test sheets at home. She took my cottage apart looking for them, but didn't find them. When I found my home turned upside down, I knew for sure that it was Nerida. She was the only one here who knew I was out with Rocky. She thought she had a free hand in finding them, but she didn't. I thought I would confront her, and she would admit it to me. I didn't think she would try to kill me."

"Miss Clay, I think we better retrieve these test sheets now before they are retrieved by someone else."

Chapter 43

Following the Chief Inspector and Lei in Rocky's Nissan, we arrive at the cottage in time to see the first light of morning on the horizon. The chaos of upturned furniture and strewn about books and pantry items surprised even the Chief Inspector.

"Why didn't you call me when you saw that?" whispers Rocky, a little offended that I wouldn't have thought of him immediately to save me from intruders.

"Now, Miss Clay. Where have you hidden the test sheets?"

"In the small room in the corner of the living room, in one of my Nan's old books. Nerida didn't find the room because the green trunk stood in front of it."

I retrieve the sheets and hand them to Mr. Brown, who holds an evidence bag open for me.

"Great. At least that is solid evidence. Hopefully, someone can interpret these for us."

"Lei can, I am sure. The horse names on these lists belong to Alan's training outfit, where we have taken blood, and I can remember all their names. You only need to work out where they race this weekend, and you'll be able to get them tested at the races."

"Does your memory also tell you where there are races this weekend?"

"No, except there is one here, the Green Bowlder Picnic Meet, but it's only a picnic race, and they probably wouldn't be bothered with that. Not enough money in this small event. They probably would focus more on the city races and interstate. And overseas betting."

"I know everything about the races," says Lei. "No need to speculate. We will raid Alan's premises at first light. I am sure they have started trackwork already, and we will bounce right into their little, or better big, scheme."

I see Rocky's eyes light up when he hears the word Green Bowlder Picnic Race Meet, but I have no clue why.

"Miss Clay, I will leave you alone now to put your life back together, but I think with your neighborly helper here, you will get that done in no time. I will need you in town later in the afternoon for a formal interview, but consider yourself ruled out as a suspect now."

"Thank you, Chief Conductor," I say and give him my best smile. "See you later then."

"I wish ... " he starts but does not finish the sentence and turns to his car. I know what he wanted to say.

Maybe he doesn't like to repeat himself, or he starts liking his new title.

The convoy of police cars departs without sirens toward the fancy horse training business. I am sure that Botox Rose, if she is already at work now, will get the shock of her life and properly guide the police in the right direction to carry out their raid.

"Let's get this organized now," says Rocky. "I'll help you, and then we can have breakfast."

George has been staying out of the way of the police and now approaches us, with a sheepish expression as if to say sorry for his slight bout of cowardice. Precious is already in the kitchen on the bench, hoping I make an interesting breakfast.

After tidying up, I brew two big mugs of coffee, and we sit down to cheese, ham, and tomato toasties and scrambled eggs.

Rocky gives me a long look across the kitchen table as if assessing my features for the first time. I suddenly am aware of my less than flawless appearance and feel the blood rush to my face.

Oh, these gray eyes! I don't want to stare, but realize that I do so want to stare that it makes my heart hurt.

"Well, little pea, I would agree with Nerida that you are skinny but not that you are ugly. In fact, I totally disagree."

I burst out laughing.

"That's the weirdest compliment I ever got. Thank you. Do I call you "pea" now, too? She said we are like peas in a pod. But I have never seen a pea with eyes like yours, so I'd rather keep calling you Rocky."

Now it is his turn to laugh and turn red. A little self-consciously, but it is still a laugh.

"How about going to the Green Bowlder Picnic Meet with me on the weekend? Pop can mind the cows and sheep, and your dog can mind the horse and the cat. What do you think?"

My heart feels the lightning bolt strike again. I probably should slow down the speed of the conversation.

"Sure, that would be lovely, if Leonard lets me go and doesn't give me extra days on call now. And I don't have anything to wear for fancy picnic meets."

"You look great as you are, but I am sure you'll find something special. I think Leonard will give you the day off, considering your success in finding the killer. He'll probably need to totally rearrange his business here because he lost not only one vet but three, Michael, Nerida, and Lei. I don't think Lei will keep working here, but you never know."

"That's true. Maybe he'll employ three more and until then I'll have to do the work of three? Oh my ... " Rocky finds this funny.

"I better go now to help Pop. He'll be wondering if the 'witch of blue wren cottage' has cast a spell over me."

He jumps into his Nissan and meeps twice. I wave after him, knowing he will be looking in the rearview mirror.

"He's such a lovely boy, your Rocky. So courteous. I will help you with some clothes for the race meet. I got some in the trunk in the little room. They were my favorites, and they have come back right into fashion now."

"Nan! Have you been hanging around here all the time?"

"Of course. That's my job as your Nan."

"Mum has packed a few dresses of mine. They might just be right for this event."

"Nah, your mum doesn't know how to dress for a picnic race meet."

"Nan, your dresses will probably all be out of fashion. I'll look like one of the girls in the movie about the Picnic at Hanging Rock."

"Nah, you won't, and the real girls didn't wear those white dresses. They were naughty girls. I should know. Just go and see what you like.

End of Book 1

Enjoyed this book? Join my newsletter for updates and the prequel to the series. Its title is "The Green Trunk".

You can download it here: https://dl.bookfunnel.com/okyivq9vrl

You can also follow the author on her Facebook page: https://www.facebook.com/mimi.singer.2024

Acknowledgements

When I first thought about writing a paranormal cozy mystery, I didn't realize how much I would enjoy sitting at the keyboard and hammering away at the keys every day until the story was complete.

I am so grateful for the input and ideas of my alpha and beta readers, whose suggestions found their way into my story. Many of the book characters' experiences may be reminiscent of some of my own, but only in the faintest possible way. Stories develop a life of their own and seem to suck ideas from here and there. When not put into the straight jackets of locality and reality, surprising things happen on the pages.

I thank my editor Roxx for going through my manuscript with the finest of toothcombs available in her toolkit without going insane.

My publishing coaches at Best Page Forward are the best. They're guiding my "Blue Wren Cottage Mysteries" series to publication. I am so grateful for you sharing your experiences.

I appreciate my family's reminders to enjoy life's simple pleasures, such as weeding the garden or brushing the cat.

About the Author

Mimi Singer, originally from Europe, has traveled to and worked in several countries. She now lives in Australia with her family and her pets. She loves writing books for children and young adults, but also paranormal cozy mysteries.

Thank you

Thank you for reading my book and spending your time with me in the paranormal environs of Blue Wren Cottage.

As an independent author, my book lives and dies by the reviews it receives receive. Please go over to the marketplace where you purchased the book and leave an honest review to help others decide if this over book is right for them.

Thank you!